ALSO BY KATHERINE ARDEN

Small Spaces

Dead Voices

The Bear and the Nightingale

The Girl in the Tower

The Winter of the Witch

DARK WATERS

KATHERINE ARDEN

putnam

G. P. PUTNAM'S SONS

G. P. PUTNAM'S SONS
An imprint of Penguin Random House LLC, New York

Copyright © 2021 by Katherine Arden
Excerpt from *Small Spaces* copyright © 2018 by Katherine Arden
Excerpt from *Dead Voices* copyright © 2019 by Katherine Arden

Visit us online at penguinrandomhouse.com

Library of Congress Cataloging-in-Publication Data
Names: Arden, Katherine, author.
Title: Dark waters / Katherine Arden.
Description: New York: G. P. Putnam's Sons, [2021] | Summary: "Stuck on a mysterious island, Ollie, Coco, and Brian must band to together if they hope to escape the creature that haunts them on both land and sea"—Provided by publisher.
Identifiers: LCCN 2021004839 (print) | LCCN 2021004840 (ebook) | ISBN 9780593109151 (hardcover) ISBN 9780593109168 (ebook)
Subjects: CYAC: Supernatural—Fiction. | Best friends—Fiction. | Friendship—Fiction. Champlain, Lake—Fiction. | Horror stories.
Classification: LCC PZ7.1.A737 Dar 2021 (print) | LCC PZ7.1.A737 (ebook) | DDC [Fic]—dc23
LC record available at https://lccn.loc.gov/2021004839
LC ebook record available at https://lccn.loc.gov/2021004840

Book manufactured in Canada
ISBN 9780593109151

1 3 5 7 9 10 8 6 4 2
FRE

Design by Eileen Savage. Text set in Dante MT Pro.

To Cassandra,
the very first fan of this series

1

SPRING IN EAST EVANSBURG, and the rain poured down like someone had turned on a hose in the sky. High in the Green Mountains, the rain turned snow into slush and turned earth into mud. It washed ruts into roads and set creeks to roaring. It sluiced down the roof of a small inn perched on a hillside above town.

The rain had begun at dawn, but now it was that long blue springtime twilight, getting close to dark, and the inn looked cozy in the soft light. The walls of the inn were white wooden clapboards, neatly painted. The roof was red metal. The sign said MOOSE LODGE, and it swung, creaking, in the spring wind.

The inn's parking lot was empty. Everything was quiet.

Brian Battersby lived in the inn with his parents. The inn had started off as a day spa, inherited from his great-uncle. But slowly, Brian's parents had turned it into a proper inn, with ten rooms. It was a Tuesday in late April, and the lodge was empty. The skiers had all left for the year. The bikers and hikers hadn't come yet. There was no one in the lodge at all except for Brian and his two friends. His parents had gone down into East Evansburg.

"We'll be back in a few hours, with dinner," they had told him. "Don't burn the place down."

"Sure," Brian had said. "No problem." But he'd gulped a little as he watched his parents drive away. He and his friends hadn't been alone in months. They'd been careful not to be alone.

They felt safer when they weren't alone.

Brian and his friends were in the main room of Moose Lodge. It was extremely cozy. There were paperbacks on shelves, magazines on tables, and a huge stone fireplace with a fire crackling.

The door was locked. They felt safe. Well. Sort of safe. They hadn't felt completely safe in months.

"Spring rain is way worse than fall rain," said Brian, shoving aside his disquiet. He'd been sitting cross-legged on the sofa opposite the fireplace, but now he dumped his book to go stand by the front window. He peered past the curtain at the big sweep of parking lot and the muddy, washed-out track of the dirt road beyond. Everything was veiled in rain, water falling like ropes and raising a mist where it smashed into the ground. He added, "Because in fall you're not even *hoping* for it to get warm and sunny. But in spring . . ." He squinted out into the twilight. Was that something moving? No, just a trick of the light.

"You're tired of winter," finished his friend Olivia Adler from another sofa, where she lounged on pillows, wrapped in a wool blanket, a book in her lap. Ollie was taller than Brian. She had big dark eyes and corkscrewing curls that stood out all over her head. She took a sip from a mug of hot chocolate, trying to nab a marshmallow with her teeth. He heard her swallow before she asked uneasily, "See anything out there?"

Brian kept watching the streaming window. "No," he said.

"I don't mind the rain," chimed in Coco Zintner. Coco always looked on the bright side. She was sitting on the floor nearest the fireplace. She was practically *in* the fireplace. She was the smallest person in the sixth grade, and she got cold easily. A stack of books teetered at her side, and she sipped at her own mug, a knitted blanket around her shoulders. Her hair, which was pinkish, was braided down her back. "It's cozy in here."

"Yeah," said Brian, a little doubtfully. They'd spent a lot of that winter holed up in cozy places. Long afternoons in the Egg, Ollie's old farmhouse. Weekend mornings in the small, neat house Coco shared with her mom in downtown East Evansburg. And plenty of time in Moose Lodge, where Brian and his parents lived.

But Brian was tired of being cozy. When you couldn't go out, places stopped being cozy and started being small. He was tired of peering out of windows and into mirrors, looking for anything out of place. Looking for danger.

The main room at Moose Lodge had white walls and old pine floors and piles of pillows on each sofa. The radiator clanked; the walls were covered with pressed flowers and dried leaves and bugs behind glass. Snug, woolly blankets draped the furniture and them. It smelled like orange oil and pine.

The only not-quite-right thing was the blanket that Ollie had used to drape the mirror opposite the fireplace. The second Brian's parents had left, she'd covered up the mirror and wrapped it in bungee cords, all without saying a word.

Mirrors, all three of them knew, could be dangerous. None of them trusted mirrors, especially not Ollie.

While she covered the mirrors, Brian had bolted the doors.

They were fine, Brian told himself. They were *safe*. Turning away from the wet window, he tripped on a pile of books.

"Ouch!" Brian hopped, clutching his stubbed toe.

"Book monster strikes again!" cackled Ollie just as Coco said, "Are you okay, Brian?" Their voices echoed in the empty lodge.

"Yes," he said, dropping with a grimace back onto the sofa. "No thanks to this stuff." He glared around at the books. Twenty or so books, divided into three heaps, one for each of them. Brian pulled the top book off his stack and scowled at it. The title was *Hauntings and Horrors in the Green Mountain State*.

"I think I read this one already," he said. "They're all blurring together."

Ollie's book was called *Giggles in the Dark: True Stories of Truly Awful Hauntings*. "I know what you mean," she said. She pulled a blanket tighter around her shoulders. "Anyway, I dunno if any of it is helpful. Like—listen to this." She read aloud:

Long ago, the Green Axe Man lived alone on South Hero Island. He used to steal other people's milk, but his neighbors were so afraid of him that no one ever said a word about it. Once, by accident, he cut his hand off with his own axe, but he was

5

so tough that he didn't care. He just stuck the axe where his hand should be. Ever after, he had an axe instead of a hand, and whenever he went out, you could hear the chopping from far away as he swung his arm back and forth . . .

"Weird," commented Brian.

"Not what we're looking for, though," said Coco.

Actually, Brian thought, none of them *knew* exactly what they were looking for. All they knew was that they were desperate to find it, and they really hoped they'd *know* when they found it.

Coco's book was called *True Tales to Make You Scream.* Slowly, she said, "Maybe no book has what we're looking for. I mean—we've been doing all this research since December, and we haven't found anything. Not even a *clue.*"

"There's something," said Brian fiercely. "Somewhere. We just have to keep looking."

He picked up *Hauntings and Horrors in the Green Mountain State* and flipped a page. Both girls fell silent. The rain wrapped them in its roar, like another blanket. If something tried to creep up on them, there was no chance they'd hear it through the sound of the rain.

Don't think about that, Brian ordered himself.

Brian's eye snagged on a new paragraph.

CAPTAIN SHEEHAN AND THE WRECK OF THE *GOBLIN*, said the heading.

The wreck of the *Goblin* wasn't what they were looking for either, but Brian paused anyway. He loved stories about boats.

In 1807, went the text, *the* Goblin *was a merchant vessel on Lake Champlain. Her master was called William Sheehan, and folk said that he was the smartest, the handsomest, and the most ruthless ship's captain between Burlington and Ticonderoga.*

But the Embargo Act of 1807 stopped his trade, and so Captain Sheehan turned to smuggling. He smuggled timber to the British fleet in Halifax and smuggled linen back. And he was good at that too.

Until the night he, his ship, and his crew disappeared.

On a foggy night in the fall of 1808, the Goblin *waited at the mouth of Otter Creek to pick up a cargo. But the revenue cutter* Fly *had been warned about the notorious* Goblin. *She was waiting. Sheehan and his men were forced to flee.*

The ships raced across the lake, into the night. The Goblin *led, with the* Fly *sailing after. All night the two ships sailed. Sheehan tried every trick he knew to lose the* Fly, *but the revenue cutter hung on.*

Finally, the fog dispersed and the moon rose, revealing a terrible sight.

The Goblin was no longer under sail. She was sinking. Bow to the sky and stern in the lake. She must have run aground, but on what? The two ships were in open water.

The Fly went closer. And closer. But before she could reach the Goblin, the smuggler went down with a gurgle. The sailors on the Fly waited to hear the shouts of survivors.

But there was only silence.

When dawn came, the Fly swept the area where they'd seen the Goblin go down.

But there was nothing. Not so much as a floating plank to show where the Goblin had been at all. Men and ship had been swallowed by the lake.

But on foggy nights, it's said, you can still see the Goblin racing across the lake. And you can still hear Sheehan cursing the Fly for sending his ship to her doom—

The lights flickered.

Brian's head jerked up from the book. Ollie and Coco looked around too, warily. The lights flickered again.

"Must be the storm—" Coco began.

And then the lights went out.

Right at that same moment, someone knocked— *boom, boom, boom*—on the door.

The three of them froze. They knew better than to scream. They stared at the door. The only light came from the fire. It threw their shadows big and strange on the walls.

Boom. This time the knock shot them to their feet and close together. Coco tripped over her pile of books; Ollie caught her, and they stood in the middle of the room, hands gripping tight.

"I didn't see anyone outside!" Brian breathed. "I didn't see a car . . ."

"There wasn't a car," whispered Ollie. "We'd have seen the lights."

"Maybe it drove up with the lights off?" whispered Coco.

Ollie glanced down at her wrist. She was wearing a watch. But it wasn't an ordinary watch. It had belonged to her mother, who was dead. Its screen was cracked; it didn't tell time. But sometimes it gave Ollie advice.

Like now.

It was glowing faintly blue, and a single word jumped on the screen in faint, flickering letters.

HUSH, it said.

All three of them went still. Brian felt sweat start on his forehead. His heart was thumping away, like a pheasant in spring. Why were heartbeats so loud? He tried not to breathe. He could feel the girls' hands sweating in his. Run away? Stay still?

The knocking had stopped. Now he heard the soft sound of footsteps. Circling the house. Going toward the big front window. *Scratch. Scritch.* Someone was scraping at the pane of glass. Brian's heartbeat seemed to rattle his rib cage. None of them moved.

The footsteps went back toward the door. Now they saw the door handle quiver. Very slowly, the handle turned downward. Down and down it went. Brian couldn't see the dead bolt in the dimness. He'd locked it, hadn't he? Hadn't he?

He could hear Coco breathing quick and shallow beside him.

The door handle was down at its very lowest point.

"Run," whispered Ollie, her hand clutching his.

But before any of them could move, a brilliant light cut through the curtains, like a car—a car coming across the parking lot. The handle stopped moving. They all stood, holding their breath.

The lights flickered. Came back on.

The door was still shut. There was no one there but them.

"I locked the door," Brian whispered. "I did. I *swear.*"

"I believe you," said Ollie. She glanced down at her watch again. Brian looked over her shoulder. So did Coco.

The watch was blank now. Just an old digital wristwatch, too big for Ollie's wrist, with a spiderwebbing crack on the screen. They were all trembling.

The headlights in the parking lot cut out. Next moment, Brian heard his parents' voices, arguing cheerfully, as his mom and dad got out of the car. He breathed again. They might have imagined the whole thing.

But he was pretty sure they hadn't.

"What was that?" whispered Coco.

"I—don't know," said Ollie.

"Saved by your parents, Brian," said Coco. "I guess that *is* your parents?"

"Yes," said Brian. They were still clutching hands.

"You don't think anything's still out there?" said Ollie. "Anything dangerous?"

"The lights came back on," Brian pointed out shakily.

Neither girl replied. He heard his mother's footsteps on the front walk. Heard them pause on the front porch. Then she came clattering in, pausing at the threshold to say something, laughing, to Brian's dad. Just like normal.

Brian's mom seemed surprised to see them all standing in the middle of the great room. "You look like baby raccoons on walkabout," she said, smiling. "I guess you got hungry?"

Brian licked his lips and found his voice. "Yeah, Mom," he said. "Super hungry."

Brian's mom had light brown skin and her eyes were just like Brian's. *Like a pond in summer,* Brian's dad would say. *When the light shines through.*

When the inn was in season, they ate whatever the restaurant was serving. When it wasn't, they ate a lot of takeout. His mom, who ran the restaurant during the season, got tired of cooking. "A break, please. I beg," she'd say, and call the Thai place or the burger spot. Everyone in town knew his mom.

Now Brian smelled something yummy. The next second, his dad came in, holding four flat boxes.

His dad said, "We met Roger and Zelda in town." Roger and Zelda were Ollie's dad and Coco's mom. "They're coming up for dinner. Brian, wash your hands, wash your ears. It's time to make dinner!"

Coco said, "Mr. Battersby—are we not eating pizza?"

Brian's dad looked at the boxes in his hands and jumped, like he was surprised. "Oh," he said. "Where did these come from?"

His dad liked to joke. So did Ollie's dad. They got along amazingly. "Ha," said Brian. "Come on," he added to the girls. "Let's wash up."

As they were heading out, he heard his mom calling. "Brian—Brian," she said. "Did you leave anything on the front porch?"

Brian stopped. Beside him, he felt the girls go still.

Brian turned around. "Um, no," he said. His tongue felt sticky. "Why do you ask?"

"Nothing, really," said his mom. "Just found this on the ground in front of the door. Thought I'd check before I chuck it in the bin." She held it up. It was a round black piece of paper about the size of Brian's palm.

Brian hesitated. Then Ollie said clearly, "That's mine, Ms. Battersby. I dropped it. School project."

"Well, great," said his mom. "Glad I could find it before it got wet."

She held it out. Ollie glanced at her watch, as though for guidance. But her watch didn't do anything, and Ollie marched over and took the black piece of paper from his mother's hand.

"Hm," said his mom, frowning at all three of them. Brian supposed they still looked a little freaked, from the darkness and the scratching footsteps. "Are you okay? Probably hungry, huh? Go get washed up. I'll set the table."

They went into the washroom. The second the door closed, Coco said, "Ollie, what's that?"

Ollie was eyeing the thing in her hand with puzzlement. "A piece of paper. Look, someone charcoaled this side. That's why it's black." She held up a black-smudged hand to demonstrate.

"What about the other side?" said Coco.

Slowly, Ollie turned it over. The back of the paper wasn't charcoaled. There were a few words written instead, in delicate, old-fashioned cursive.

bell, it said. Then, *dog saturn day flower moon.*

And then, *Consider yourselves warned.* —S.

One shiver chased another up Brian's spine.

"Who is it from?" whispered Coco. They looked at each other. "Is it—is it him?" Her voice went shrill. When they first met him, the smiling man had called himself Seth, and he had seemed nice. He wasn't, though. Not at all. Coco's finger traced the spidery cursive *S.*

Another knock broke the silence of the bathroom. All three of them stiffened, glancing instinctively at the bathroom mirror. But nothing moved in the mirror but them. The knock had come from the front door. Again? But the lights were on.

Brian felt the hair rise on his arms.

The front door creaked. They all held their breath. And then a chorus of adult voices—"So glad you could make it, come in, come in . . ."

They relaxed a little. "It must be your parents," said Brian. "Dinner party time."

Ollie was still considering the smudged black paper, turning it over in her fingers. "What do you think this means?"

"It's a riddle," said Coco. "And I guess a warning, like it says." People often underestimated Coco. She was very small, and her eyes were pale blue and watery. She cried a lot. She was possibly the bravest person Brian knew. "The smiling man likes games and riddles," she added. Coco would know. She'd played him at chess once, with Brian's life as the prize. "Any guesses?"

They shook their heads. Brian frowned. There was something tickling the back of his brain. Something about bells. Bells and dogs and spots. Black spots? But it slipped away before he could grasp it.

Coco said, "Maybe our parents would know?"

The other two looked at each other. Their parents didn't know anything about the smiling man.

Brian silently ran over a speech in his head. One he'd thought out a million times since that fall. Since the three of them—and their entire sixth grade—had disappeared into a foggy forest.

Hey, Mom and Dad. Remember when our whole class vanished for two days and then reappeared? When no one remembered what happened to us?

But me and Ollie and Coco lied. We remember what happened—

"No," Ollie broke in fiercely. "We can't tell them. It's too dangerous. The smiling man messes with adults too. If our parents believe us, if they help us, it might put them in danger, and we are *not*"—here she stopped to glare around at her friends—"putting my dad in danger. Or anyone's parents."

"They'd want to know," Coco pointed out. "If we were in danger. They'd *want* to help."

"If they even believe us," retorted Ollie, "how would it go? 'Hey, Dad, you know that there's this other world lurking behind mist and behind mirrors? A ghost world? Well, there's someone out there who wants to trap us there, behind the mist, forever. Got any advice?'" There was a brittle, fearful edge on her voice. Ollie had lost her mother in a plane crash; Brian was pretty sure that for Ollie the thought of losing her dad too was scarier than any ghost world.

Coco said, "We don't have to tell them where the riddle is *from*. Or tell them why we want advice. We could just say it's a school project. I mean, it wouldn't even be a stretch. They've seen our books about ghosts everywhere . . ." She trailed off. She was still carrying her current book, her place carefully marked. It was only one of the millions they seemed to have read since the winter. In not one of them was there a single clue about how to beat the smiling man.

"Not even then," said Ollie. "What if they help us without knowing and that's enough to put the smiling man onto them? We'd be cowards to tell them. Asking for help, *putting them in danger*, just to make ourselves feel better."

"But I don't want to be brave," said Coco. "I want everything to be all right again. What if we can't fix it by ourselves?"

"Nothing will be all right if they get hurt," returned Ollie hotly. "Do you want lights going out and things scratching at our parents' windows? What if our parents disappear?"

"We *can* fix it by ourselves," broke in Brian. "I know we can. Eventually. We just have to keep looking."

Neither girl said anything.

"We can," he repeated, a little angrily. The last time they fought the smiling man, Brian hadn't helped much. Coco and Ollie had outsmarted the bad guy, but Brian hadn't even been there. He'd been trapped in a lodge that had become a strange, vast hall of doors, none of which led where he expected them to. The endless doors had kept him away from his friends until it was all over. It hadn't been his fault, it had been the smiling man's trick, but still. The memory didn't feel good. Actually, more than a few of his daydreams since then had been of him, Brian, swooping in at the last second and singlehandedly saving Ollie and Coco.

After all, why not? He was smart and brave and strong. His parents were proud of him for a *reason*. He was strong enough to keep his parents safe, and to keep the girls safe too.

"Ollie's right," he said to Coco. "I don't think we should tell anyone."

When he took the paper from Ollie, the black circle left sooty smudges on the tips of his fingers.

"I think we should," said Coco. "It's all a game, remember? He's probably *expecting* us not to tell anyone. We need to do something he won't expect." Coco was shy and Coco was gentle, but in the last six months, she'd gotten a lot better at standing up for herself. "We're not getting anywhere with books. Guys, what just happened? The paper is a warning? A warning about *what*? We don't know what he's planning! We—maybe we can't do this on our own."

Ollie had her mouth open on a reply, but a bellow from the great room interrupted. Ollie's dad, who had an enormous, cheerful voice, was calling, "Hey, you three mice! Are you asleep in there? If you want dinner, now's the time. Pizza's getting cold!"

"Um," said Brian, sidetracked.

"Come on," said Ollie. "I'm starving."

Coco scowled. She had taken the black circle, was holding it between her hands. "I still think we should tell them," she said to Ollie's back.

"I don't," said Ollie, heading decisively for the door.

Coco looked at Brian. "We might not have that much time left," she said. "We need help, Brian."

"Yeah," said Brian. "I do know that. But, Coco, what if—what if telling them just means he nabs them instead of us?"

Coco bit her lip. The two of them exchanged grim looks. They were passing through the great room by then, and Brian turned, half reluctantly, to look at the mirror that Ollie had covered up, the second they were alone.

"I can't think, otherwise," Ollie had told them, shuddering. *"Sometimes, with mirrors, I imagine—I'm almost sure I see—things moving in there. At night. I keep thinking, if I go too close, it'll pull me in."*

How much more of this can we take? Brian wondered.

He followed Coco, clattering, to dinner.

2

BRIAN'S PARENTS AND Ollie's dad, Roger Adler, were standing around the island of the big, echoing kitchen that produced all the meals for the lodge. The adults had steaming mugs of something spicy-smelling in their hands. They all turned around as the kids walked in. Brian almost stopped in his tracks, because just for a second, the three adults looked at them with identical worried expressions.

"Hey, guys! Zelda's working late," said Mr. Adler, smiling. Zelda was Coco's mom. Just like that, all three worried expressions were gone. Brian wondered if he'd imagined them. Ollie's dad was wearing a tangerine-colored flannel shirt. He had the same eyes as Ollie: big and dark and kind. "She says to start eating without us," Mr. Adler added.

"Good," said Brian's dad. "You all must be hungry."

They sat around the kitchen table and helped themselves to pizza. There was pineapple and bacon for Brian's dad and for Ollie. There was three-cheese for Brian and Coco. All vegetable for Brian's mom, who liked broccoli on pizza, and a squash-and-mushroom-and-rabbit one for Ollie's dad, who always got the weirdest pizza on principle.

"Amazing," said Mr. Adler, chewing. "We need to hit White Rock Pizza more often. What do you think, kids? Hope you didn't drink *too* much hot chocolate."

"We didn't," said Coco, swallowing before she answered. Coco was very polite. "The pizza is yummy." She was still frowning, her eyes downcast. Probably thinking of the smiling man. Or that black circle.

Black circle . . . Why did that ring a bell? Black circle, black spot . . . which had something to do with . . . bells?

No, gone again.

Brian, eating and thinking, felt his mom's gaze, like an itch on his forehead. He wondered what she was worried about. It couldn't be about him, could it? He'd tried so hard not to worry his parents.

But what if they'd noticed something anyway?

Or had they seen something? Driving up? A cold clutch of fear hit his stomach. What if they'd seen whatever was outside? What if it came back that night and scratched on their window?

"Okay," said Ollie's dad. "New joke: what did the fisherman say to the magician?"

Mr. Adler loved awful jokes. Brian's dad frowned with concentration. Everyone else at the table groaned. The dads had a shared interest in bad jokes. They were a terrible influence on each other.

"Don't know," said Brian's dad. "What?"

"Pick a cod, any cod," said Mr. Adler happily. They both laughed.

Brian's mom sighed.

"All right," said Brian's dad. "I've got one. What did one ocean say to the other?"

"Ooh," said Ollie's dad. "Lemme think . . ."

Brian sighed. "They just waved," he said.

"Oh, of course they did!" said Ollie's dad, with delight.

"So," said Brian's mom, breaking in. "Ollie, I hear you are a great softball player."

Ollie swallowed her bite. "I was," she said. "Or, am, I guess? I didn't join the team this spring."

Ollie had thought about joining, Brian knew. She'd quit softball after her mom died but had been slowly getting back into her old hobbies. She and Coco played chess sometimes after school. But sports had seemed a little silly when they were desperately researching how to save themselves from a monster. Brian had just finished the worst hockey season of his life. It was hard to play hockey when you were scared all the time. And now they had this black circle with the riddle on one side. A warning, if *S* was to be believed.

What do we do?

A knock boomed against the front door. All three kids jumped. Brian saw his mother's eyes narrow. He tried not to look nervous. "Hello?" called a voice from the entryway. There was a thump of someone pulling off boots, and then Coco's mom came in, fair hair sticking to her face with the wet outside. "Wild night, huh? Hi, sweetie," to Coco. "Hey, everyone." She kissed the top of Coco's head and took a seat to a chorus of hellos. Since Ollie, Brian, and Coco had become friends, their parents had too.

"Have some pie, Zel," said Mr. Adler. Coco's mom passed a plate.

"Hi, Mom," said Coco, swallowing.

Coco's mom started on her pizza. She was a reporter for the *Evansburg Independent*. Her hair, neatly braided, was blonder than Coco's, and she wore a woolly sweater instead of a flannel shirt. Her nose was freckled, her expression serious. "This is fantastic. Now, I need an honest opinion here. What do you all think about boats?"

"Huh?" they all said.

"I like boats," said Brian, after a pause, relieved to talk about something not related to himself and the girls. Maybe it would stop his mom from looking worried. "I've been in canoes a lot, and I sailed last time we went to see my cousins in Kingston." Brian had been born in Jamaica; his family moved to East Evansburg when he was a toddler.

"I've canoed a lot too," chimed in Ollie. "No sailing, though."

"Why do you ask?" asked Brian's dad. "I used to sail all the time as a boy." His expression went far away for a second, and Brian figured he knew what his dad was remembering: all those trips to Kingston, when Vermont was dark and icy cold. He wished he was there now, but they'd already gone for a week in February. Somehow, terrible mysteries didn't seem like they could get ahold of you under the warm sun, in the middle of sun-bright water.

"Oh, that must have been lovely," said Coco's mom to Brian's dad. "I'm not thinking of anything that remarkable, though—take a look at this."

She pulled a brochure from her bag and handed it around.

Brian examined it. On the front was a drawing of a bright green creature that looked like a cross between a dinosaur and a dragon. It was swimming, with a big toothy smile.

Over this picture were the words

MEET CHAMP: THE LEGENDARY MONSTER OF LAKE CHAMPLAIN.

Brian snorted. Champ was the Vermont Loch Ness monster. There were lots of Vermont restaurants and car washes called Champ's. Ollie peered over his shoulder. "I met Champ at a baseball game when I was five years old," she said. "He was furry and green and wore a striped jersey." Champ was, among other things, the mascot of Vermont's minor league team.

"Well," said Coco's mom. "If you open the brochure, there's this guy, Dane Dimmonds—he owns a boat named *Cassandra* on Lake Champlain. Sails out of Burlington. He has a business called Champ Tours. Takes out tourists, tells people the history of the lake, points out places that are associated with legends of the Abenaki. *And* places where people have reported Champ sightings. Supposedly. Anyway. I'm going to do an article for the paper about Mr. Dimmonds. I'll spend a day on the *Cassandra*, take his tour, and write about it. But the boat's pretty big—I thought we could all go.

Roger?" This was to Ollie's dad. "Make a day of it. What do you think, kids? Win? Amelia?"

"Yes, for sure," said Mr. Adler. "This weekend?"

Ms. Zintner nodded.

"I don't think we have anything else going on," said Mr. Adler. "Ollie?"

"Yeah!" said Ollie. "Sounds fun." She eyed the black, streaming windows. "I mean, if it gets warmer and stops raining."

"For sure," said Ms. Zintner, and shivered too. "But the forecast is good this weekend." She smiled at Ollie, and Ollie smiled back, a little uncertainly. Ollie's dad and Coco's mom liked each other. They *like* liked each other. Ollie hadn't been okay with that at first, but she was trying really hard. So was Ms. Zintner. Sometimes they tried so hard that it was awkward. But at least they were trying.

Brian was delighted, imagining a day of open water and bright sun. Where nothing could get at them, nothing could knock on a locked door and scratch and leave creepy paper behind. A day of *fun*. He couldn't remember the last time he'd had fun. But he looked at his own parents and found them exchanging glances. "I'm sorry," said Brian's dad. "We have plans this weekend."

Brian stared. He didn't know about any plans. And he *really* wanted to go sailing.

"I didn't know we had plans," he said.

"We have to uncover the shrubs," said his mother very firmly. "And weed the garden beds. Summer season will be here before you know it. And your grades are slipping. You need to stay home and study."

Brian bit his tongue. It wasn't like his grades were *bad*. Neither were Ollie's and Coco's. But grades were another thing that all three of them had let slip that winter. Brian didn't want to stay home and study. He wanted to go sailing.

"I'll study extra hard the day after—" began Brian, but even as he said it, he knew that it was no good.

"We'll talk about it, don't worry," said his mother in the voice that meant *no*, and took a very decided bite of her pizza.

The conversation turned to a different topic, and Brian was left with Ollie and Coco shooting him sympathetic looks over the table.

3

COCO KEPT THE black circle. "I have some ideas," she said, holding it by the corner as though she didn't want to touch it. Even after the girls left and the circle was gone, Brian could still almost see it, floating in front of his eyes like a sunspot. Sun—he wanted to be out in the sun, on open water, where nothing could get him, or scare him, or snatch him.

"But why can't I go sailing?" Brian asked his parents. "It's not like I'm failing school. It's not even like my grades are bad! B's aren't bad."

"They're not what you're capable of," pointed out his mother. She was making tea with pale green leaves. The sweet, grassy smell filled the kitchen. "Besides . . ." She hesitated and glanced at Brian's dad.

"Brian," said his dad. "I'm not sure those girls are good for you."

This was completely out of the blue, and Brian was left gaping, speechless. Finally, he managed to sputter, *"What?"*

"It's like this," said his mom. "You started spending time with those girls in the fall. And since then your grades are worse, you're over at Olivia Adler's house every afternoon if you don't go to Coco's or bring them here. And you're *different*. You used to love hockey, and this season you didn't even seem to care how the team did. You ignore your old friends. And you only read books about ghosts. Scary things. You used to love fiction! What changed? Brian, we're worried."

I'm worried too, Brian thought. Part of him wanted to confess everything in one big speech. *Remember when we disappeared last autumn . . . ?* But Ollie's sharp question was clear in his mind: *What if he nabs them instead of us?* For a minute he was so torn he could hardly make himself talk.

"It's not the girls," he managed at last. "Stuff is weird in my life, but it's not them."

"What is it, then?" asked his mother. "Brian, *what's wrong?*"

Brian opened his mouth, closed it again.

Answers, lies and truths, shot through his brain. But in the end, all he said was, "Things are weird right now. The girls are okay. They understand. That's all."

"How are things *weird*?" Brian's dad asked.

"I—things have been weird since we, um, had that thing. In the fall," said Brian. "Where we all went missing." Which wasn't even a lie, in its way.

"I knew it," said his mother. The look she turned on him was about eighteen times more worried. Her knuckles were white on her teacup. "I knew they spray the corn here with awful pesticides, chemicals, it's probably affecting your mind—that's what the scientists said—"

"Erm, no," said Brian. "No, that's not it. It's just weird, not being able to remember."

That was a complete lie, and he felt himself cringing as he said it.

"Yes," said his dad, in a softer tone. "It would be."

Brian added, "I promise I'll do better in school and sports. Just—I love boats. Like you, Dad. Born to sail. Can I please go sailing? Please?"

A long silence as his parents looked at each other again.

Then his mom said, "It might do you some good—a break. All right. You can go. But, Brian, if something's wrong, you *tell* us. And you need to spend some more afternoons at home, until your grades improve. And also help us finish weeding on Sunday. The summer garden won't grow itself."

"Okay," said Brian. Words—a million more words—seemed to collect in his mouth, but he couldn't bring himself to say any of them.

What if he nabs our parents too?

Just like Ollie, Brian would do anything to prevent that. Anything at all.

Well, he thought, turning up the stairs for his own room, peering out into the streaming, wet April dusk before he did. At least he was going sailing.

If nothing happened first.

What did that circle mean?

4

THE NEXT MORNING dawned gray, and the sun looked like a half-drowned face staring out between thick, wet clouds. Brian left for school, his head stuffy with tiredness.

The rain had slacked off since the night before, but only a bit. Waiting for the bus at the corner of Crossett Hill, the hood of his rain jacket over his head, Brian eyed the sky. Would they go sailing after all? It was already Wednesday. Hopefully the weather would improve before the weekend.

The bus came, and Brian got on. The driver was Ms. Hodges, like always. Brian checked every time now. Just to be safe. The day everything had changed, their bus driver had been different. Was Ms. Hodges looking at him strangely? No, he was imagining it.

He looked up and down the rows. Usually Ollie got picked up before he did, but Ollie wasn't there now. Late, maybe. Ollie was late a lot.

Phil Greenblatt was sitting three rows from the back, scribbling. Brian went over. "Hey," he said.

"Hey," said Phil, distracted. He was finishing his English homework, a little wild-eyed. That day's English homework was getting graded.

"Can I sit down?" Brian asked. "I won't bug you." The bus jolted into motion, and he hung on to the seat back.

Phil glanced up, looking surprised. Brian used to sit with Phil all the time, although these days he mostly sat with Ollie and Coco. "Um, yeah," said Phil. "Sure."

Brian sat down, feeling awkward. Weirdly, because he and Phil had been friends since preschool.

Phil didn't say anything else, just bent his head to his homework. Phil Greenblatt had curly, floppy brown hair and a big, nice face, with little eyes like two raisins right in the middle. He was the goalie on their hockey team. Brian and Phil used to hang out all the time. Best friends.

Brian hadn't known that things had gotten awkward between them. It wasn't awkward playing hockey, of course, or talking about the team. But now, just sitting together on a bus, with no hockey practice coming up and no one else to talk to, Brian realized that he didn't know what to say. To Phil Greenblatt, of all people. It made him sad. No wonder his parents were freaked out.

His eye fell on Phil's homework. It was an essay question about a poem by Robert Frost. Vermont kids read a lot of Robert Frost, since he wrote his poems in and about Vermont.

Brian had read the poem yesterday afternoon and written his essay right away. English was the only class where his grades hadn't slipped. He loved reading; at least *that* hadn't changed. Even if he was tired of ghost stories.

I have been one acquainted with the night, the poem began.

I have walked out in rain—and back in rain . . .

Brian actually wasn't *trying* to look over his friend's shoulder at his homework. *What do you think the poem means?* the essay question went.

But Brian did happen to glance, and he caught sight of the first lines of Phil's essay:

The poem "Acquainted with the Night" is about being alone, it said. *The narrator walks back and forth, in the dark, and doesn't talk to anyone. Maybe because the narrator has a secret, a big bad secret, and he can't tell anyone, so he just walks alone in the dark—*

"Hey!" said Phil, slamming a hand down, hiding the beginnings of his essay. "Don't look at my homework!"

Brian put his hands up. "I *wasn't*," he said. "I was just—"

"You were looking," said Phil, and then his hand shook or something, because then his whole heap of messy papers went tumbling, *whoosh*, onto the floor of the bus.

Instinctively, Brian bent to help pick them up. "Here," he said. "This one went under the seat. I'll grab—"

Phil said, "No, wait, *don't*."

But Brian had already put his hand down to the paper. He saw the one on top and froze.

It wasn't homework at all.

It was a drawing of a scarecrow. But not just any scarecrow. This scarecrow had a stitched-on scowl and stabbing garden rakes for hands and a long, ragged black coat. Brian knew this scarecrow's name.

"Jonathan," he whispered. He picked up the paper without thinking. The page was covered with drawings of scarecrows. Some with sewn-on grins, some with gaping scowls, some with pumpkin heads, some with heads made of burlap sacks.

Phil snatched the paper back. His face was very red. "Dude," he said. "You shouldn't just grab at private stuff. That's mine! You don't have any right to look at it!"

Brian said, "But, Phil. I thought you didn't remember."

"Remember what?" Phil demanded suspiciously.

Brian stared. "October! The smiling man!"

"I don't know what you're talking about," said Phil.

"But," said Brian, confused. "Where'd you get all this—the ideas for all those?" He pointed at the sketches.

Phil was still glaring, his mouth shut up tight. Then he said, "Just dreams, that's all. Just dreams."

Brian licked his lips. "Bad dreams?"

He thought Phil wasn't going to answer. Then he said softly, "Yeah. The worst dreams. The worst dreams in the world."

Phil shoved the drawings under the rest of his messy heap of paper and then went back to his essay. Brian didn't know what to say. He'd been sure—he'd been *completely sure*—that what had happened to them in October had just disappeared from everyone else's minds. That he, Ollie, and Coco were the only ones struggling, the only ones in trouble.

And if they weren't? What did that mean?

———

The rain stopped before recess, and a watery sun broke through the pearly spring clouds. Brian texted Ollie and Coco as he was heading out of English class.

Maple tree.

He didn't need to say anything else. The maple tree stood at the far end of the playground, right up against the woods that surrounded Ben Withers Middle School. They liked to meet in its branches when they needed to have a private conversation.

Brian had a bad morning. He was tired. The jolt of seeing Phil's drawings had brought back memories— rake hands grabbing, scarecrows bending nearer with their blank, unchanging smiles. Being stuck in a corn maze, held tight by scarecrows, watching Ollie climb, desperately, and knowing he couldn't do anything to help her.

He'd tried to talk to Phil again after class, but Phil wouldn't. He just put his head down and went to the library. And wasn't that weird too? Phil Greenblatt, choosing to spend recess inside?

Frowning, Brian went out into the playground, crossed to the maple tree, and shimmied up. Ollie and Coco got to the maple tree right after he did. Coco had to jump for the lowest branch, while Ollie could just reach up and grab it. But they both climbed to Brian's perch and settled in.

Coco said breathlessly, "I think I got part of it—the circle, I mean. The message."

"Yeah?" said Brian, with sudden hope. "Which part?"

"Well, the last two words, *flower moon*, if those are actually a phrase—well then, flower moon is a thing. Every full moon used to have a name," explained Coco.

"I looked it up. September is Harvest Moon and October is Hunter Moon and January is Wolf Moon, for example."

"Which one's Flower Moon?" asked Ollie.

"May," said Coco.

They looked at each other. May 1 was that Friday.

Suddenly Ollie said, "Saturn day—Saturday? Hang on." She pulled out her phone. "Yes," she said, scrolling. "Saturn's day—or Saturday—is the only day in the calendar still dedicated to its original Roman god. Saturn is the god of generation and of dissolution and—" She broke off.

"It's a time, sounds like," said Brian. "*Saturn day flower moon*. A Saturday in May . . . ? But what about the rest? I don't know anything about bells—or dogs. Do you?"

The girls shook their heads.

"Let's stick together in safe places on Saturdays in May," said Coco.

Ollie nodded instant agreement. "Good thing we're going sailing on this one," she said. "Far from creepy farms and creepy lodges."

"Yup," said Brian. He told them what he'd seen in Phil's homework on the bus that morning. "I asked him if he remembered—October. But he only said that he'd been having nightmares."

"Pretty specific nightmares," said Ollie. "If he drew all those scarecrows."

"But I thought—I thought no one remembered!" said Coco. She was the highest in the tree, peering down at them, like a bird, through the branches. "What if it's not just us?"

"It's us," said Ollie firmly, leaning against the tree trunk. "We saved everyone else. We're the ones the smiling man hates. It's us."

"But," said Coco, "how do we know for sure? Brian, Phil is *your* friend. You could talk to him."

"Yeah," said Brian. "But didn't we decide that talking to people put them in danger?"

"Not if he's already drawing pictures of scarecrows," said Coco. "He's already *been* in danger. Maybe he still is."

"But Phil doesn't want to talk to me. He blew right by me earlier."

"Well," said Coco, "you hang out with us now, and Phil was mean to me in the fall. Maybe he thinks you're not his friend anymore."

That hadn't occurred to Brian. Of course he was Phil's friend. But—

"We're not his friends," broke in Ollie. "Coco, he was a bully."

"Maybe he feels bad about it now?" said Coco, a little uncertainly. Coco always tried to see the best in people.

Hastily Brian said, "Let's just try and solve the black circle first. We have a warning. We need to know what it means. What do *bell* and *dog* mean?"

The girls looked at each other. Slowly they shook their heads.

"But we'll figure it out," said Ollie determinedly. "We *will*."

5

THE DAY THEY went sailing, Brian's parents dropped him off at the Egg in the middle of the morning. The Egg was Ollie's house. It was a farmhouse, built in 1890. There was a foundation stone in the basement that said so. It was called the Egg because Ollie's dad, who loved bright colors, had painted it all the colors of an Easter egg. The outside was purple, with a bright red door.

Brian's mom pulled up outside the door and looked at him searchingly. "Brian," she said, "we don't *want* to control who your friends are; we're not ogres. You don't think we're ogres, right?"

"Um, no," said Brian.

"But," his mother added, "we want what's best for you. So after this sailing trip—you hit the books, okay?"

"Okay," said Brian, wondering what his mom would say if she knew that his sudden fascination with ghost stories wasn't just him going through a phase. If she realized how hard he'd been hitting the books. Just not the right books.

"Love you," she said.

"I love you too."

He went into the Egg and was instantly swept up into a whirl of activity. Mr. Adler, like always, had gone really overboard in his trip preparations. He was filling a giant hamper of food. Brian went over for a peek—and maybe to grab a snack. Mr. Adler had made shortbread cookies, each one shaped like a brontosaurus, with the legs cut into a flipper shape, and iced in green.

"I only had dinosaur cookie cutters," he said. "But I think they look like lake monsters, don't you?" He winked and didn't say anything when Brian snitched a cookie. Besides the cookies, there were sandwiches, neatly wrapped and labeled. Brian saw egg salad (ew) and ham and Swiss (yum) and Ollie's favorite, peanut butter and jelly. There were chips and carrot sticks and hummus and stuff to drink.

"Thanks, Mr. Adler," said Brian. "This looks awesome."

He went upstairs to where Ollie was packing and Coco advising. She was sitting on Ollie's beanbag chair, watching the chaos, munching toast with strawberry jam. Brian joined her, eating his cookie.

"Rain gear," said Ollie, shoving distractedly through her stuff. "Woolly hat, sunglasses, sunscreen, swimsuit . . . Hi, Brian."

"Hi," said Brian.

"You know," said Coco to Ollie, "it's nice out. I dunno if you'll need a woolly hat. Also the lake's *cold*. It only finished melting a couple of weeks ago! Are you really planning to swim in it?"

The girls both looked as happy as Brian felt. To be doing something other than huddling at home, researching and worrying.

"You never know!" crowed Ollie, sounding just like her dad. "We might."

Brian felt himself start to grin. It felt like a holiday. And, yeah, sometimes the girls drove him up the wall, and he'd gotten pretty tired of just hanging out with the two of them all winter, but they were still his best friends in the world.

"*I* know," said Coco firmly. "Swimming is not a thing in May."

"Swimming," said Ollie, "is a thing whenever."

They piled into Susie the Subaru, Mr. Adler's car, the back end stacked high with bags and coolers.

"Anyone think we'll meet Champ?" said Coco's mom from the front seat, once they'd gotten on the highway.

"Maybe," said Ollie's dad. "What do you guys think? Is Champ a leftover dinosaur?"

"I don't see how a dinosaur can be left over," said Coco. "Left over from what?"

"I think," said Ollie, "that someone in Vermont back in the day went to Scotland, learned that *they* had a lake monster, and got jealous."

"Or that," said her dad. "Now I'm trying to imagine who gets jealous of some other country's lake monster."

"A Vermonter," said Brian decisively. "We're all a little weird."

"Okay," said Mr. Adler, after they'd parked the car and gotten out at the marina. "The boat is called the *Cassandra*, and she's the one with—"

"The giant lake monster painted on the side?" asked Ollie, pointing.

"Um," said Mr. Adler, staring. "Um, yup. That looks like the one."

Brian followed the direction of Ollie's finger. He saw a big boat, white except for the smiling green dinosaur with flippers. The dinosaur was eating what looked like an ice cream cone. Over the picture in big letters were the words *MEET CHAMP*.

On the stern was painted the boat's name, *Cassandra*. There were two people on deck. One of them was a man that Brian had never seen before. He was wearing a flannel shirt under a green jacket, with a knit beanie and gray hair sticking out from under it. Brian supposed that he was Mr. Dimmonds, the owner of the boat.

The other person was Phil.

Brian and Phil saw each other. They both stopped dead in surprise.

Mr. Adler was marching ahead, wearing his own beanie (that he'd knitted himself) in every color of the rainbow. He was loaded down with coolers. "Hello!" he called.

"'Lo," said Mr. Dimmonds, in a thick Vermont accent. "Pleased to meetcher."

Coco's mom said, "Mr. Dimmonds? I'm Zelda Zintner. Sent by—"

"Know who you are," said Mr. Dimmonds. "Gonna ask me questions, aren'tcher? This is my nephew Phil."

"Of course we know Phil!" said Mr. Adler happily. "I didn't know you were related. Hi, Phil."

"Hi, Mr. Adler," said Phil. He was looking uneasy. Like he wasn't sure if he was happy to see them.

"How long have you had your tour boat, Mr. Dimmonds?" asked Ms. Zintner. She'd already pulled out a little reporter's notebook, ready to scribble.

Mr. Adler started hauling all the coolers onto the boat. "Watch your step, guys," he called back over his shoulder. Although she climbed like a cat, Coco could be unbelievably clumsy on the ground.

"'Bout twenty years," said Mr. Dimmonds. "You kids ready to see the beastie today?"

"Champ, you mean?" asked Ms. Zintner. She was scribbling notes, with an eyebrow raised.

"Champ, yup," said Mr. Dimmonds. "Silly name for an old thing like her."

"*She* might be a boy," pointed out Ollie.

There was a twinkle in Mr. Dimmonds's eyes. "She might indeed, little lady, but I guess it's hard to know. Come aboard, and I'll tell you about it and show you round the *Cassie*." At Ms. Zintner's puzzled look, he added, "The *Cassandra*! My pride and joy." He patted the boat's mast.

"Eeek!" yelped Coco, and Mr. Adler lunged just in time to keep Coco and the bag of sandwiches from going into the lake. Coco, Brian noticed, had been watching Phil and not looking where she was going. She obviously still wanted to ask questions.

But Phil doesn't remember. It was just dreams. He said so.

Yeah, so? another part of himself said. *He might have been lying. How many times have you fibbed this winter? About what happened, about what you are doing or plan to do?*

Brian belatedly realized that if you told a lot of lies, even if it was for a good reason, like trying to keep people safe, it started to get hard to trust that *other people* were telling the truth.

He felt a jab of hatred for the smiling man. Hanging around somewhere in the dark, frightening them with stupid riddles written on black spots and ruining their lives for fun.

Well, he can't ruin anything today, Brian thought.

They piled onto the boat. Coco was still eyeing Phil. Phil looked nervous. Coco looked distracted. Ollie and her dad had to rescue Coco and the snacks multiple times from oblivion.

The *Cassandra* was a thirty-foot sailboat. The deck was white, the railings white too, with storage lockers along the sides and two inflatable lifeboats. The wheel was near the back, and Brian itched to touch it.

A mast soared over his head.

Suddenly Brian made a decision and veered straight over to Phil. He was tired of being awkward. It felt like letting the smiling man win. "Hey, dude," he said firmly. "Awesome to see you."

"Hey," said Phil. He had both hands in his pockets. Brian had never seen Phil looking so self-conscious.

"I didn't know you were coming," said Brian.

"Well, the *Cassie* is my uncle's boat," said Phil. "I help out a lot on weekends. He taught me to sail." Phil puffed a little with pride.

Brian said, "I'd like to learn more about sailing. I've only been once or twice. In Jamaica."

"I can tell you some stuff," said Phil, looking happier.

Brian caught Ollie glaring from across the boat. Phil had been mean to Coco last fall, and Ollie hadn't forgotten. He saw Coco mouth *Be nice* at Ollie and then come up to them with Ollie trailing. Coco was more forgiving than Ollie. "Hi, Phil," Coco said.

"Hi," echoed Ollie grimly.

Phil went bright red. "Hi, guys," he mumbled. He was playing with something in his pocket.

Coco had her mouth open to say something else, when Mr. Dimmonds came up behind Brian. "Well, hello, you three," he said. "Guess y'already know my nephew Phil. Ready to be sailors?"

"Yup," said Brian, with slightly excessive cheer. He was determined to have a perfect day. "What do we do first?"

Mr. Dimmonds said, "Better stow your stuff first." He had an eye on their hampers of food. "Glad you've brought your own grub. People these days, pah! Most people expect you to do everything for them. Everything!" He spat over the side of the boat. "Phil!" he added. "You can show your new shipmates the ropes. Take 'em down to stow their bags. We'll cast off in just a few."

Phil still looked tense. But he said, "Okay. This way." He led them toward the back of the boat. The *stern,* Brian remembered. There was a steep staircase there, almost a ladder. "Down here." Phil climbed down the ladder, calling over his shoulder, "Just watch your step, okay? These steps are slippery. You can stow your bags." He pointed to some racks.

"Okay," said Coco. She heaved her bag.

"Wow, you're stronger than you look," said Phil. "I mean, that is—" He bit his lip.

Coco said, "Well, I like to climb a lot. Do you think I could climb the mast?"

"Yeah," said Phil, looking surprised. "But it's hard. My uncle only let me do it once. And you need safety equipment. A harness. Want to see?"

"Sure," said Coco, and followed him instantly back up the ladder.

Ollie, looking annoyed, threw her own bag into the luggage rack. "I don't get why she's even being nice to him. He was *so mean* to her in October."

"Yeah, and then he got turned into a scarecrow," said Brian. "She probably feels bad about that. You know Coco. She *wants* to be everyone's friend. We weren't that nice to her either, once."

"Coco makes me feel like a fiend sometimes," Ollie admitted. "Like a big meanie. She's just—nice. It's not an act, it's who she is. She's going to ask him about scarecrows and the smiling man, isn't she?"

Brian sighed. "Probably. Can't stop Coco when she decides to do something. I wish we knew what the black paper meant."

"Me too."

———

When Brian and Ollie got back up to the deck, the boat was already moving. "Look!" said Mr. Dimmonds from where he stood, steering. "See those whitecaps, out on the lake? We've got some breeze today!"

Brian looked. The lake was glassy blue, with white streaks where the wind had beaten the water all foamy, like eggs. Clouds darted across the milky spring sky, but the sun was warm when he put his face into the light.

Mr. Dimmonds said, "You kids want to help me steer?"

"Yes!" said Brian instantly, and went over. Ollie came too, but slower. She was watching Coco and Phil, who were standing next to the mast, talking.

Mr. Dimmonds was watching them too. "Good to go, my dear," he called to Coco. Coco was already wearing a harness. She clipped it in, put her feet on the rungs and shimmied up like a squirrel. Phil watched in surprise. Mr. Dimmonds whistled. "Very impressive, young lady," he called, and Coco waved from the top of the mast, smiling.

When she got back to the ground, Phil blurted out, "Hey, I'm sorry I was—I was mean this fall." He tripped over the words.

A few months ago, Brian was pretty sure that Coco would have ducked her head and said *no problem*. Now she looked Phil in the eye. "You made me cry," she said.

"I—" Phil turned bright red. "I know. I'm sorry. It wasn't right."

"Why did you do it?" she asked.

Phil said, "To make myself look cooler. I'm sorry again. Look, you don't have to forgive me or anything. You don't, um, owe me anything. I just wanted to say it." He started to turn away.

"I don't know if I want to be friends," said Coco honestly. Phil stopped. "But I'm not mad at you anymore. I'm not good at staying mad at people." Coco was watching Phil like a cat at a mousehole. "You can't be mad at someone after the amnesia thing that happened to all of us."

Phil's face changed. He ducked his head. "Right," he muttered. "Right, the amnesia thing."

"Yeah," said Coco. "So weird that no one remembers anything."

"Yup," said Phil, paler than ever. "Really weird. Hey, um, yeah, I'll be right back."

He hurried down the ladder into the hold again, like he was trying to get away from them all. Coco turned to Ollie and Brian. "Doesn't remember anything?" she said. "Yeah, right."

"He sure looks like he remembers something," said Ollie reluctantly. "But I don't know—"

"Hey!" said Mr. Dimmonds. "Hey, let's sail the boat here! This lady won't steer herself. Gotta hoist the sail!"

Their conversation broke up. With Mr. Dimmonds's help, the sail whizzed up the mast, filling like a cup with the quick May wind. "Hey, Brian," called Mr. Dimmonds, "come and take the wheel. Show me what you got, son."

Coco, who had no interest in sailing boats, went over to the bench seat in front. Ollie's dad was already sitting there, staring out at the water. His hair was sticking up with the wind. Coco sat down next to him and got out her sketchbook. Mr. Adler grinned at her. Ollie wandered over and sat down on her dad's other side. They looked like a family. Brian was glad to see it. He knew it hadn't been easy for Ollie, letting new people in. She loved Coco, and she even liked Coco's mom now, but she still missed her own mom and the way her family used to be. Who wouldn't?

Ms. Zintner was standing by the wheel with Brian and Mr. Dimmonds. She had her notebook out. Brian only vaguely heard her ask, "So, how many guests do you take on the lake every year?" He didn't catch Mr. Dimmonds's reply at all. Brian's eyes streamed with tears from the sun on the water and from the cold wind blowing in his face.

In the bow, Ollie and her dad started unpacking a late lunch. They laid the sandwiches out neatly on the padded bench. Brian realized that he was hungry. After a few more minutes, he left off steering and went to join the girls. He snagged a ham and Swiss sandwich. Ollie's dad, chewing his egg salad sandwich, smiled at Brian, got up, and went toward the back of the boat to join the grown-ups. Coco was still sketching. She hadn't taken a sandwich. She wouldn't let anyone see her drawing.

Phil came over. "Can I have a sandwich?" he asked, a little uncertainly.

"Sure," said Brian. "Ollie's dad always overpacks. The ham and Swiss is really good."

Phil leaned over to grab a sandwich, hovering between the PB&J and the ham and Swiss. But before he could choose, he frowned, his hand not quite touching either. "Who is that?" he asked.

Brian followed the line of Phil's gaze. Phil was staring down at Coco's open notebook. Brian craned his neck and bit his lip. Coco's sketch took up the whole page. Brian recognized the face she'd drawn. It was a face that had stuck tight in his memory. A narrow face, sharp-nosed and big-eyed, with a wide grin. A grin that could look friendly or terrifying, or amused, or kind. Fair hair falling over the forehead.

The smiling man . . .

Coco was better at drawing than Phil. Brian had recognized the scarecrow Jonathan when Phil drew it. But it felt like Coco had done a tiny magic trick, to lure some essence of the smiling man, laughing and charming, mean and old, onto their boat with them. Like the face would start talking.

Ollie had seen it too. "Cover it up," she said flatly, gone pale.

Phil said, settling on a PB&J, "Weird, you know that guy too? He's cool, huh?" He unwrapped the sandwich and took a large bite.

Ollie, Brian, and Coco all swiveled around to stare at him.

"You remember him?" said Coco. "The smiling man? From the farm?"

Phil just looked puzzled. "I—no," he said. "I met him this week, actually. In town. Um, just in the general store. He wasn't weird or anything. He was nice . . ." Phil broke off. "Why are you asking? How do you know him?"

"Phil," said Brian. He heard his voice shake, just a little. "Phil, listen carefully. When you met him this week—what did he say to you?"

Instantly, Phil's face, which had been interested and curious, shut down. "Why do you care?" he said.

"Because that man, the smiling man, is *bad*," said Ollie.

"Whatever," said Phil. "He was nice to me. He gave me . . . Well, it's none of your business."

"*Nice* to you?" snapped Ollie. "He's the one that turned you into a scarecrow, Phil."

Phil shot backward, dropping his sandwich. The PB&J fell splat to the deck. "No he didn't! That didn't even happen! It was a hallucination!"

"We were all there," said Coco gently.

"Shut up!" Phil snapped. "Just shut up! It didn't happen!" He was backing away as he spoke. Suddenly he spun and hurried away down the ladder. As he did, a sudden squall of misty rain blatted down out of nowhere, brief but intense, wetting the deck, wreathing them in a soaking-wet cloud. Coco yelped, and there was a splash. They all dived for the sandwiches, to keep them dry.

In the second of confusion that followed, they heard Mr. Dimmonds's voice from the wheel. "Wow, take a look at that island!" he said. "And—I can't believe I'm saying this, but I have no idea which island it is. Man, the ole brain box must be going."

6

THE SQUALL OF misty rain lifted as fast as it had come, and the *Cassandra* sailed on under an untroubled sky. Coco, dead white, was staring over the rail of the boat. "Coco," said Ollie. "Where's your notebook?"

Coco's breathing was not quite steady. "I threw it in," she said. "My picture, of the smiling man—I could have sworn—I could have been wrong, but . . ."

"What?" said Brian.

"It winked at me," whispered Coco.

They stared at each other. "We have to go after Phil," said Ollie instantly. "Figure out what he knows."

"Wait," said Coco, looking shaken. "We can't just all stampede after him. Brian should go. They're like hockey bros together."

"This is not the time to be delicate! What did the smiling man tell him?" said Ollie. "It's important! Maybe really important!"

Mr. Dimmonds's voice broke in again. "Man, kids," he said again. "Get a look at this island!"

This time the three of them turned around. Coco's mom and Ollie's dad were standing at the boat's railing, staring. Mr. Dimmonds tied the wheel and went to join them. "Beats me," he said. "I can't for the life of me figure out which one it is. We're well south of Grand Isle, and the heading's wrong for South Hero. It's not on my chart. A mystery island!" Enthusiasm flushed his face. "Let's check it out."

"Wait," said Ollie sharply. "Mr. Dimmonds, I'm not sure that's a good idea."

Brian had been thinking the same thing. It was a Saturday in May, the smiling man had been lurking around Evansburg, they had just passed through a freak rainstorm, and the mist of it still clung to their hair. Brian wanted *no part* of a mysterious island.

"Seriously," said Brian, improvising fast. "It might have shoals, right? Shallow water. I don't see any buoys, Mr. Dimmonds."

"That's true, son," said Mr. Dimmonds. But he looked eaten up by curiosity.

"Hey," said Mr. Adler. "The kids are right. I'd rather you not risk shoal water, Dane." Ollie shot her dad a grateful look.

"Oh, all right," said Mr. Dimmonds, looking grumpy at having to agree. "Mutiny, is it? Can't kill me, though, no one's given me the black spot, have they? Have they?" He creaked out a laugh at his own joke and went to drop the anchor.

"Wait," said Ollie slowly. "Did you say black spot?"

"Well, yep," said Mr. Dimmonds, looking a little taken aback at whatever he saw on Ollie's face. "Old pirate custom. Giving someone a black spot."

Brian, Ollie, and Coco all exchanged glances. "What does it mean," Brian asked, "when you give someone a black spot?"

"Well," said Mr. Dimmonds. "Generally speaking, it means death. To the person who gets it."

Brian's breath hitched. Ollie, very slowly, put down her sandwich. A line appeared between Coco's eyebrows. Mr. Dimmonds didn't notice. He'd headed back to the stern of the boat, whistling. The wind brought a springtime earth smell from the land. The island had a rocky top and a fringe of trees around the sides, like an old, bald man. Brian hardly noticed.

Death . . .

"Death?" whispered Coco. "A threat? Or just another stupid game?" Her hands were trembling. "What did he tell Phil? What did he give Phil?"

"Who knows," said Ollie. "My watch hasn't said anything. We need to ask him. Now."

Mr. Dimmonds was flipping furiously through his charts. "I can't find this sucker *anywhere!*" he said, with an irritated wave at the island.

Ms. Zintner was shooting pictures of the island, clearly planning her article in her head.

"It's probably Pine Island, just mislabeled," Mr. Dimmonds muttered.

Ollie's dad was peering at the chart too. "Pine Island is three miles east, looks like," he said.

"Well, what else could it be?" asked Mr. Dimmonds reasonably.

Mr. Adler didn't have an answer. The seagulls circled, screaming, keen for his ham and Swiss sandwich.

"It's today," said Ollie abruptly to Brian and Coco.

They both turned to look at her.

"Has to be," she added. "Remember the words? *Bell*, it said. Then, *dog saturn day flower moon*. Well, today is a Saturday in May. Saturn day flower moon. And black spots—a black spot is something that pirates do—people on *boats*. Like us. Today. And the smiling man was in Evansburg this week. We have to talk to Phil."

Her watch beeped softly. They all turned to look. ~~FISH~~, the watch said nonsensically.

60

"Are we eating fish for lunch?" Coco asked, looking puzzled. "Don't eat it?"

"No, we aren't," said Ollie. Her face was strained. "Is Phil still below?"

In the background, Coco's mom was talking to Mr. Dimmonds. "So, have you seen the—um—lake monster before?" she asked.

"Three times," he said. "On'y three, but it's more than anyone else, I reckon."

"Can you tell me about those encounters?" asked Coco's mom.

"Oh, yeah," said Mr. Dimmonds.

"Hey, guys!" called Ollie's dad from his seat in the front. "Did you hear the joke about the ducks?"

They didn't reply.

"You're right, Ollie," said Coco. Her face looked strained. "Let's go talk to him. Right now."

Mr. Adler said, "What did the farmer say when he let his ducks out?"

They were crossing the deck. "I—don't know?" said Coco, her voice unsteady.

"Release the quacken!" cried Mr. Adler, and busted up laughing.

Phil wasn't below deck. He'd come back up in all the confusion, holding a fishing rod, and they found him standing at the back of the boat, casting his hook in the water, attached to a lure that sparkled strangely in the afternoon sun.

"Hey, buddy," said Brian. "What are you doing?"

"What does it look like?" said Phil, leaning on the back rail, looking elaborately casual. "Fishing. You guys are all acting weird."

"Well," Mr. Dimmonds was saying, "I only ever saw her in the mist. On foggy mornings, or mornings with fine rain. Like we just had, lotta squalls work up out here. And this one time, I'm in the boat in the fog—" Mr. Dimmonds paused dramatically. "And I see a shadow."

"A shadow," repeated Coco's mom gravely.

"Yup," said Mr. Dimmonds. "A twisty shadow. Under the water."

"And then?" said Ms. Zintner.

"I—well, just a shadow," said Mr. Dimmonds in annoyance. "But bigger than anything that lives in the lake, I'll tell you that!"

Ms. Zintner sighed. "Of course."

"Phil," said Ollie. "We need to know—"

"Go away," said Phil, turning his back to him. "You guys don't care; don't pretend you care. I don't have to talk to you at all."

Abruptly Coco turned toward the adults and called, "Mr. Dimmonds, do bells have anything to do with time? Like a time of day?"

Mr. Dimmonds said, "Hm, well—that's how you used to tell time on board sailing ships, warn't it? A bell every half hour."

Bell, thought Brian. But Coco had already taken the question out of his mouth. "When is one bell?" asked Coco.

"Depends on which watch it is," said Mr. Dimmonds. "Day was broken up into six, ya know. Six watches, with eight bells each."

"Do—any of the watches have anything to do with dogs?" Ollie broke in.

"Well—there's a dogwatch," said Mr. Dimmonds. "That'd be the fifth one. One bell in the dogwatch is . . . about four thirty, I'd say. Right around now, come to think of it."

Brian's stomach clenched up. The three exchanged glances. Ollie was looking down at her watch. ~~FISH~~. "Phil needs to quit fishing," she said.

But Phil had caught something while they weren't looking; he was struggling with his reel, his rod bent almost double.

"Whoa!" said Mr. Dimmonds, hurrying over. "Did you catch a shark, son?"

"Phil, let it go," said Brian.

"No way!" said Phil, panting. The fishing rod was about to be yanked out of its holder. Phil held on with both hands. Mr. Adler leaped to help. So did Mr. Dimmonds. "Phil," Coco said. "Please, whatever it is, let it go."

"No way," said Phil again. "It's the biggest thing I've ever caught!"

"Good lord," said Mr. Dimmonds, feeling the weight on the fishing pole. "Here, lemme . . ." They all strained together.

"Let it go!" chorused Ollie, Coco, and Brian, just as a slim silver thing, maybe four feet long, popped out of the water thrashing, swung aboard, and landed on deck, still thrashing. It was—not as scary as Brian had been expecting.

Coco said shakily, "Is that a fish?"

"Kind of skinny for a fish, isn't it?" said Coco's mom.

"Looks like—" started Mr. Dimmonds.

"A snake," said Phil, staring. "Looks like a snake. A water snake?"

"Throw it back!" snapped Ollie.

"Hang on: I didn't know there were water snakes in the middle of Lake Champlain," said Mr. Adler. "Cool!" He was eyeing the thrashing silver creature with interest. It twisted back and forth on the deck.

Phil reached down to grab the thing behind the head, but Ollie lunged forward and hauled him back. "What?" demanded Phil. "What's your problem?"

"It has *fangs*," said Ollie.

Death, thought Brian. "Stay away from it!" he cried.

Phil jerked back. The fangs were small. But they were definitely there. Thin black liquid was oozing out of one of them. It had teeth like needles. Fiercely the snake thing bit at the deck. Then it lunged at Ollie. She leaped back. "We need to get rid of it!" she cried.

Phil looked around at their frightened faces and said, "Whatever. I caught it, and I'm—"

The silver thing lunged, mouth wide, going for Phil's hand.

Would have gotten it too. If Mr. Adler hadn't put his whole arm in front of Phil, shoved him unceremoniously to the deck, and gotten bit himself instead, straight through the skin between his finger and thumb.

Right at that second, there was a giant crash from somewhere underneath them, and the *Cassandra* rocked hard, nearly going over, like an upended toy. They were all thrown, sliding, to the deck. Ollie's scream, "Dad!" was lost in the confusion.

Death, thought Brian. *Oh God.*

7

CHAOS EVERYWHERE, BUT only for a couple of seconds. The *Cassandra* was a good boat; the violent rocking stopped. The water snake lay limp on the deck, its scales sparkling. Mr. Dimmonds had stepped hard once on its neck where it joined the frilled head, breaking the spine. Its color was already beginning to fade.

Ollie had hurled herself down to kneel beside her dad, who'd gone pale. Two black punctures showed on his hand, running a little stream of dark blood. "Dad," said Ollie. "Dad, are you okay?"

"I think so," said Ollie's dad. "It doesn't feel great, but I don't think it's bad." He was sweating. "Here, help me up. Phil—" Mr. Adler turned toward him. "Don't you *ever* go grabbing at snakes again, do you hear me?"

Phil was white-lipped. "Yes, Mr. Adler," he said. He looked stricken.

Ollie looked at her dad's hand, then back to his face. "I'm okay, hon," he said, seeing her expression. "I'm just fine. Little love bite, really. But—Zelda—I'm afraid we're going to have to cut the boat trip short. Just—to be safe. I'd like to have a doctor check it."

"Yes," said Coco's mom. "Yes, for sure. We'll turn around right now. Put out a distress call, have an ambulance meet us . . ."

Brian had learned about snakebites in the Scouts, although he hadn't learned about any silver water snakes with frilled necks on freaking Lake Champlain. He said, "You ought to cover it up, Mr. Adler. And save the snake, if you can, to show the hospital."

Mr. Adler nodded, grimacing. His hand probably hurt him.

"I bet the *Cassandra* has a first aid kit," said Phil. "Somewhere."

"Yeah," said Mr. Adler. "Yeah, that'd be good." His hand was puffing up around the fang holes.

"Dane would know," said Coco's mom, straightening up. "Dane?"

They all looked around. Mr. Dimmonds was nowhere to be seen.

"Did he fall into the water?" asked Coco.

Mr. Dimmonds popped out of the stairway like a gopher out of a hole, holding a tape measure and a digital scale. He wore an expression like it was Christmas morning. He didn't seem worried about Ollie's dad. He hurried to the water snake, pulled it straight, and began to measure it, muttering to himself, "Four foot—no, make it four foot two . . ."

"Dane!" snapped Ms. Zintner. "Can't that wait? You have an injured passenger. Where's the first aid kit?"

"By the wheel," said Mr. Dimmonds absently. His gaze was still fixed on the snake.

Brian ran to get it. Phil was looking at Ollie's dad with a sick, guilty expression. "Hey," he said. "Hey, I'm really, really sorry."

"It's okay," said Mr. Adler. His forehead was covered with fine drops of sweat, and his breathing was shallow. *His hand must really hurt,* Brian thought. "Totally fine, son."

"Dane, we need to get back to shore," said Ms. Zintner, just as Mr. Dimmonds said, "This is *it*!"

No one understood. "This," said Mr. Dimmonds impatiently. "This is Champ. A new species. Unknown in the lake. A snake. A *lake monster.*" He picked up the dead thing with an expression of reverence.

Brian was pulling out the first aid kit, only half listening. At least he could bandage the punctures . . .

Ms. Zintner said, sounding outraged, "I—you—Roger is hurt. That thing—*bit him*. Never mind what it is! We need to call 911 and to get back to shore!"

"I'm okay, Zelda," said Mr. Adler. "But yeah, I think we might have to wait on science, Dane, I'm sorry. Can we get this boat moving?"

Brian knelt down by Ollie's dad, with the first aid kit in his hands. He'd found the disinfectant, the gauze pads, the scissors. Ollie was next to him. She was still sickly pale. "What do we do about snakebites?" she said urgently. "I read that you're supposed to suck out the venom?"

Brian shook his head. "That's a myth," he said. "You bandage it, keep the—the limb elevated, and go to the hospital."

As he said that, Brian happened to glance up from where he was cutting a gauze pad to fit the punctures. Mr. Dimmonds was *not* instantly grabbing for the radio, calling 911, and starting the sailboat's motor.

"He'll be okay for half an hour, won't you, Roger?" said Mr. Dimmonds. "I've never *seen* anything like this little guy before. Besides, there's no venomous serpents on the water in Vermont. I should know. Been here twenty years! And Vermonters are tough—he'll be okay."

Ms. Zintner's mouth pressed into a long, thin line. She got to her feet. "Dane," said Ms. Zintner. "You are going to put away your specimen, call 911, and *get us back to Burlington,* please. *Right now.* Or by God, I will write such an exposé of the safety protocols on this boat that you will never get another tourist on here ever again."

Mr. Dimmonds's mouth opened and shut. First, he looked shocked, and then he looked annoyed. "Come on, Zelda," he said, like she was only joking. "Be a good sport. Thirty minutes won't matter! I need to do some quick measurements of the lake where we found this thing! Temperature, depth, take a sample . . . Feel free to call 911; we'll get underway in just a few. Doing all right, Roger?" he added to Ollie's dad. "You'll manage, I'm sure. I just need to test . . ."

He hurried down the stair-ladder before Coco's mom could say anything else. She was staring after him in disbelief.

"Jesus," she muttered. "I'll have to get on the radio, Roger. We'll have a rescue helicopter out here before you know it." She hurried.

A steady beeping had started from somewhere. Brian hardly noticed; he was carefully bandaging Mr. Adler's snakebite.

"Guys?" said Coco.

No one answered. Brian and Ollie were bandaging. Phil had gone over to try and help Ms. Zintner with the radio.

"Guys!" said Coco, at the top of her voice. They all turned to look at her. She was peering over the stern of the boat, frowning down at the water. "Guys, the motor is gone."

"*What?*" said Ms. Zintner, and went to join her daughter. "Oh my God."

Brian finished taping. A bandage wouldn't do anything about the actual snake venom, though. They needed a hospital. Ollie was holding her dad's unbitten hand. He'd managed, with Ollie and Brian helping, to get himself to one of the padded benches in the front of the boat. He sat down. He was kind of grayish, Brian thought. That couldn't be good. "Way to keep your cool," Mr. Adler told them. "So proud of you guys. We'll be back in port in a second."

Then he closed his eyes.

"Mr. Adler," said Brian, suddenly alarmed. "Ollie, I think—I think it might be better to keep him awake. Mr. Adler, don't go to sleep."

Mr. Adler's eyes opened again, and he gave them both a twitch of a reassuring smile. "Don't worry, Ollie-pop," he said. "M'here. I'm right here . . ."

His voice trailed off. In the little silence, the beeping filled the deck. "What does that sound mean?" asked Ollie. Her voice was small and thin.

"It's the pump," said Coco's mom, peering at the electronic displays near the boat's steering. Brian twisted around to look at her; she sounded like she didn't quite believe what she was saying. "It's the boat pump—it's pumping out water. We're—the boat—it has a hole in the side. Where the motor—the motor was, I suppose . . ."

"The motor?" asked Brian. "A hole? How? We've just been sitting here—"

"Something knocked it off," said Ms. Zintner. "A rock . . . ?"

Ollie broke in, her voice loud and worried. "Zelda, did you call 911 already? And *where* is Mr. Dimmonds?"

"Where's Phil?" Brian added.

"He went down below to talk to his uncle. I tried using the radio," said Coco's mom. "But—it was weird, actually, I—"

She broke off. Below their feet, in the cabin under the deck, someone screamed.

Brian shot to his feet. "I'll go," he said. "Ollie, you okay?"

She nodded once. Brian ran for the ladder steps that led to the hold. Behind him, he heard Ms. Zintner asking, "Does anyone's phone work?" Brian flicked his own phone out as he ran.

NO SERVICE, said the phone. Shouldn't they have service? Even a little? One bar? And if they didn't . . .

He went down the steps, calling for Phil. It wasn't hard to find him. Phil was standing right there in the cabin under the deck, near the stairway. Water surged and sloshed around his ankles. *The boat's leaking,* Brian thought. *But how? We didn't hit anything.*

Somewhere, he heard the loud whine of motors churning. Not the boat's motor—no, that motor was definitely gone. It must be the pump motors, trying to get the water out.

They weren't succeeding, though. Even Brian, whose knowledge of boats wasn't enormous, could tell that there was no way they were getting all that water out. It was nearly past their knees; a gusher was pouring in.

"Phil!" he said. And when Phil didn't respond, he shouted again, *"Phil! Hey, I'm right here!"*

Phil turned around. He didn't say anything, just stared at Brian as though he didn't quite recognize him. Brian said, "It's not safe down here. Phil, there must be a big hole. The water's getting in."

Still Phil didn't say anything. What was wrong with him? Brian felt himself getting annoyed. Now was not a good time to panic. "Phil, where's Mr. Dimmonds? Where's your uncle?"

Phil didn't say anything, but his eyes went again toward the giant hole in the stern, about where the motor had been. Water sloshed, freezing, around Brian's ankles.

Brian asked again, his voice going squeaky, "Phil, where is he?"

"Gone," said Phil. His voice was a weird, dull croak. "It—it *took* him."

"Phil, *what? What took him?*"

"Dunno," whispered Phil. A little snot ran down his face, but he didn't seem to notice. He looked like a mouse under a cat's paw. Frozen. "Something. A thing. A *huge* thing."

Brian was starting to shiver, his legs numb from the knee down. The lake water was frigid. "Okay," said Brian, not knowing exactly what to say. "Okay—okay, we'll figure it out on deck. Phil, let's just grab our bags and—"

But he broke off. He'd seen, just for a second, something moving in the water. Just a flash, there and gone, under the surface. "Phil," whispered Brian. "Phil—back up. Come on, let's go back up. The *Cassie* is sinking."

Phil didn't move. He was staring down at the water around his knees, as though hypnotized. Brian had to reach and grab him and pull him backward toward the ladder. "Phil, come *on!*"

Another movement: unhurried, sinuous, there and gone in the water. Brian, cold with instinctive fear, pushed Phil ahead of him, up the ladder to the deck.

A splash behind him. A plop. A groaning of metal as though—as though something big was trying to get into the boat. Or get farther into the boat.

Metal shrieked.

Brian turned around.

And saw—a mouth. Rising out of the murky, swirling water. A giant pink mouth, wide open, packed with teeth as long as his forearm. It seemed to hover right behind them, over the churning water. Brian screamed and hurled himself up the last steps, expecting with each step to feel teeth meet in his leg. But instead there was only another splash; he risked a quick look back from the top of the ladder. The—the thing—was gone. As though it had never been there.

The water below looked waist-deep now. Their bags, full of all their gear, were floating already in the surge. And . . . and there was Mr. Dimmonds's blue-striped beanie, floating too.

Brian shuddered. As he watched, the beanie sank. It had tooth marks in it.

Ms. Zintner was still at the radio when they got onto the deck. She swore at it. "The radio's out," she said. "I'm not sure how . . ."

"Phones?" demanded Brian, still short of breath and shaky. "Does anyone's phone work?"

Coco shook her head. Ollie had her head bent, talking to her dad, maybe trying to keep him awake, but she shook her head briefly too when Brian glanced her way.

"Where's Mr. Dimmonds?" asked Coco.

Brian swallowed. "Look, guys, it wasn't a rock that took out the motors. It was—"

"It was a monster," said Phil, in the first words he'd spoken since Brian hauled him out from below. He was shaking violently. His teeth chattered.

Ollie's head lifted. Coco pressed her lips together.

Ms. Zintner frowned. "Right," she said. "I know it was unsettling, that snake biting Mr. Adler, but you guys need to keep it together. We'll be all right if we just stay calm. You kids stay on deck. I'm going to go down below and see about Dane . . ."

Brian met Coco's eyes and shook his head.

Coco instantly planted herself in front of her mom. "Mom, you can't go down into the hold. Brian, how big was it?"

"Big," said Phil.

Coco's mom looked perplexed. She finally said gently, to her daughter, "I realize that something bad probably happened in the hold. But I need to see if Dane is okay."

"He's not okay," said Phil, in a strange, harsh voice.

Coco spoke over her mom's shoulder to Brian. "What was it?"

"It looked—it looked like the water snake that we caught," said Brian. "Except it was bigger. It was a *lot* bigger."

"Like baby T. rex and momma T. rex?" said Coco. "In *Jurassic Park*?"

"Um, maybe," said Brian. His thoughts felt chaotic and also too slow, like he was thinking through mud. It had been so big. "Something like that."

"Kids," said Ms. Zintner. "I appreciate that you are frightened and that this is an emergency, but I am sure there is a better explanation for all this than *dinosaurs*. Now, what we all need to do is—"

She was interrupted by a huge crash from below. The boat shook. And then another crash. There was the shriek of ripping metal. The boat rocked, sloshing them all with freezing water.

Phil's eyes went wide. His nose was running again. "It's coming!" he yelled. "It's trying to get in!"

Even Ms. Zintner looked uneasy now.

"What—" said Mr. Adler weakly. His face had gone a nasty green-gray color. "What's that noise?"

"Nothing good," muttered Coco.

The boat heaved. Metal groaned.

Brian didn't know what to do. Except . . . his eyes went to the island, less than a hundred yards away. Did they have a choice? He didn't think so. "We need to get off this boat," he said. "Phil—do you know where the lifeboats are?"

Phil pointed. Brian saw them, tucked neatly under the boat's railing: bright yellow, two of them, inflatable.

Coco said, "Don't you think getting into a rubber lifeboat might be kind of a bad idea if there's a monster in the lake?"

Brian was thinking fast now, his head clearing. "*We're* going to be in the lake pretty soon ourselves if we don't do something," he said. A huge thump came from below, as though to punctuate his words. "We just—we just need to make the—the snake *think* we're still on the boat. Give ourselves time to paddle to the island."

"How do we do that?" demanded Phil, sounding as breathless and frightened as Brian felt. "We don't know how it thinks! If it thinks!"

Brian wasn't sure either. Coco tugged her lower lip. Coco's mom had gone back to shouting into the silent radio. The *Cassandra* was so low in the water . . .

"Two lifeboats on the *Cassandra*?" Coco asked Phil suddenly.

Phil eyed her. "Yeah, but so? We don't need two. We'll all fit on one." Under their feet the boat tilted, and they all staggered. Freezing water sloshed over their shoes. Behind him, Brian could just hear Ollie talking to her dad, quietly and steadily, not paying attention to what they were doing, *trusting* that he and Coco could figure something out . . .

"We can launch a decoy boat," said Coco. "Like in chess. A feint. Launch one boat, empty, on the side away from the island. Put the boat in the water with a lot of splashing. At the same time launch *us* in the other boat, very quietly, on *that* side." She pointed again.

The rock-crowned green island, the one that didn't have a name, stood quiet, with little wavelets just breaking around the boulders at its foot. "To the island," added Coco.

"And what if the monster doesn't take the decoy?" said Phil.

"Do you have a better idea?" Coco asked.

Phil's shoulders slumped. "No."

The deck was tilting noticeably; they all had to hold something to stay upright. The back of the boat was sinking faster than the front. Water heaved and foamed around its gashed stern.

"*Hurry,*" said Brian. "Phil, do you know how to launch the lifeboats?"

"I—yes?" said Phil, but he didn't sound certain, at all. "At least, my uncle—" His voice wavered, and he tried again, sniffing. "My uncle showed me. Once."

That didn't exactly sound like enough training to Brian, but it was what they had. "Okay," he said. "What do we do?"

"This way," Phil said. He and Brian ran for the lifeboats.

"Mom," Brian heard Coco say, just as her mother slammed down the radio for what had to be the twelfth time. "Mom, we have to get off the boat. The boys are launching the lifeboats—the *Cassandra* is sinking. Can we bring the radio? In case it starts working?"

Ms. Zintner stared at her daughter, a little wild-eyed. Brian realized, with a creeping, not-so-nice feeling in his stomach, that he and the girls had been in more tight, scary corners than the grown-ups had in the last couple of months. Maybe they were more used to it. Maybe *they* knew best. Since Brian felt like he hardly knew anything at all, it wasn't a comforting thought.

The life rafts hissed as they were inflated, and Brian saw Coco's mom take a deep breath. "Okay," she said.

"You're right. You're right, hon. Let's get off this boat. I'll pack up the radio."

The deck was tilting more steeply now. *Like the freaking* Titanic, thought Brian. As fast as they could, he and Phil were loading the decoy boat with coils of rope and an anchor, to make it splash as though it held people.

"We'll need supplies for the real lifeboat," said Brian.

Phil shook his head. "A lot of supplies were down in the hold," he said.

They grabbed what they could. Some emergency blankets. A pair of emergency whistles. The first aid kit. It didn't seem like much. *But we won't be on the island long,* Brian consoled himself. Someone would see them; there were boats all over Lake Champlain. They just had to get there safely. He and Phil dragged the decoy to the lake-facing side of the sinking *Cassandra,* ready to slide it into the water.

Ollie was pulling on her dad's hand. "Come on," she said. "Dad—Dad, please. You have to get up. Try. We can't stay on the boat . . ."

"Yeah," said Mr. Adler. He was looking even more greenish now, Brian thought worriedly. He stumbled to his feet. His hand was swollen, and black stuff still leaked out of the punctures from under the bandage. His eyes were half closed.

Coco's mom ran to help. Between her and Ollie, they got him in the boat. Brian yelled, "Phil! Now!"

Phil gave him a sickly grin, and the two of them launched the decoy lifeboat. It landed with a splash. For a second it looked like it wouldn't move at all, just hang out beside the boat and not do them any good. But Phil had a long pole—maybe from the sails—and he pushed the decoy life raft out from the boat's shadow, just far enough for the wind to pick it up.

Silence. Stillness on the water. *It's not going to work,* Brian thought with sinking heart. The snake wasn't going to take the bait. Maybe it was a *smart* lake monster who would just wait for them to launch their real life raft and then lunge for it.

And then there was a sudden boiling froth of water under the decoy raft, and the whole thing went flying into the air. A snapping mouth attached to a glittering silver body came flying up after it.

Phil was staring at it, eyes enormous. Brian had to yell, "Phil!"

Phil came running. Together he and Brian and Ollie shoved the real lifeboat into the lake. It wasn't hard. The stern of the sinking *Cassandra* was more or less on a level with the lake by then. Phil jumped in after.

They pushed away. Brian and Ollie, who had done the most canoeing, each grabbed a paddle and started rowing them toward the shore. Coco's mom was white as a sheet. She hadn't said anything when she saw the creature, just hustled them faster into the boat. She was holding on to Ollie's dad. Phil and Coco were staring behind them, looking for signs of disturbance in the water.

"Take it easy, Owl," said Brian to Ollie. "Try not to splash. Maybe it's like a shark. Sharks come to splashing."

Ollie swallowed hard and nodded, her knuckles white on the paddle. The island got closer and closer. Brian had a vague impression of gloomy pine trees running down to a pebbly beach. The trees were clustered so close that you couldn't make anything out of what lay behind them. A wind riffled the trees and water. The island looked like a locked room. Brian couldn't see any signs that humans ever came there. No jetty. No boat dock. No beach, no picnic table, no path.

He swallowed hard.

Phil yelped and pointed. Brian whipped around just in time to see a silver gleam in the water. At the same moment, Ollie's watch beeped. From where he was, Brian could just read the word on the display.

FAST.

He and Ollie started paddling just as fast as they could, strokes evenly matched as they raced toward land. Brian wasn't sure they'd make it. They were close; the shadows of pine trees, stretching long, were just falling on them. But the snake was *fast*, and going faster every second. Its silver body caught the light, where its frilled head just crested the water.

Then the lifeboat bumped onto rocks. Brian and Ollie both jumped out at the same second and grabbed the gunwales of the lifeboat to pull it up the bank. "Phil! Coco!" snapped Brian. "Come on! Get out! Pull!"

They all jumped out, except for Ollie's dad, and the five of them pulled together. Five feet. Four . . .

A dripping silver head, a mouth crowded with teeth, rearing up out of the water. The head was bulging and barnacled, the eyes huge and filmy and blank. The mouth opened wide. "PULL!" screamed Ollie, and they heaved the boat up the beach, just as the teeth slammed shut with the sound of a metal door, only a few inches from the back of Ollie's jacket. The teeth caught the edge of the inflatable life raft and shredded it.

But they kept hauling anyway, panting, scrambling, cold sweat in their eyes, until the boat was as far as it could possibly go up the stony slope. There was a grinding, slithering sound behind, and Brian turned.

The lake monster had disappeared. It was like it had never been there at all. Lake Champlain sparkled, untroubled, beneath the last of that day's sun.

"Oh my God," said Coco's mom.

"Come on," said Ollie, her face set hard with determination. "We need to make a fire, signal a boat . . ."

"No," said Coco's mom. "Look."

There was a good-sized pine standing sentinel on the edge of the beach. On the side of the trunk facing the water, someone had carved, deeply and skillfully:

MAYE GOD HAVE MERCI ON YER SOULES.

They stared, and no one said anything at all.

8

THEY JUST STARED at the carving in the tree. Ollie's dad was the first to move, trying to get up from the bottom of the lifeboat. Ollie instantly turned away from the carved trunk and knelt beside him. "Ollie," he said. His breath wheezed. Even the gulls weren't crying now. "What's happening?"

"We're on the island," said Ollie. "We got off the boat. It was sinking. There was—well, I don't know what it was. Sort of like a big version of the snake that bit you. It sank the *Cassie*. But that doesn't matter. We're getting off this island as soon as we can. We'll take you to a hospital."

He nodded but didn't answer. His eyes drifted shut.

Coco's mom picked up the portable radio. "Mayday," she said. "Mayday. Require immediate assistance."

Silence. Not even static. Just silence.

"Look," said Coco suddenly. She stooped and brushed a litter of pebbles and pine needles from below the carved tree.

There, in the dirt, was a hard brown dome. Coco dug all around it until she revealed, unmistakably, the eye sockets and brow ridges of a skull.

She let it go abruptly and stepped back, wiping her hands on her damp jeans.

Behind them, they heard Ms. Zintner's voice. "Mayday, Mayday . . ."

"We're in trouble," said Brian, and Coco nodded, biting her lip. "What should we do?" she said. "I don't know anything about islands."

Brian tried to peer deeper into the woods. No luck; the forest was too dense. He could only see a few feet. The ground sloped steeply up. There were no paths. Maybe a few bare spaces between the trees, where the pines crowded out the undergrowth, but that was all.

Brian turned away from the forest. The lake glittered like a monster's scales in the afternoon sun. The water was still now, except for a few tiny whitecaps whipped up by the wind. As though neither the *Cassandra* nor the lake monster nor Mr. Dimmonds had ever existed.

Phil was staring out at the water, his arms wrapped around himself. Coco went over to him. "Phil," she said. "I'm really sorry. About your uncle."

"He was my favorite uncle," said Phil. He wiped his nose on his sleeve.

Brian had been feeling angry at Phil. For fishing, for not listening to them. Now he was just sad. Mr. Dimmonds was dead. Mr. Adler was hurt. So what if Phil had met the smiling man and somehow that meeting had led to all this? It wasn't Phil's fault. How would he even have known? It was so, so easy to trust the smiling man. Brian went over to Phil too. "Buddy," he said. "I'm really sorry."

Phil shook his head and didn't answer.

Coco's mom had finally put the dead radio aside. She pushed her fair hair off her face, eyes slitted with frustration. Ollie was trying to make her dad more comfortable. She'd dug an emergency blanket out of the first aid kit to put around his shoulders. He was still sitting in the damp raft.

"How are you doing, Ollie-pop?" said Mr. Adler, not sounding so great. "I'm okay. How are you, Zel? That was a pretty quick exit off the boat, wasn't it?"

"We're fine, Roger," said Coco's mom. She put a hand on his forehead, looking worried. "We'll get out of here really soon. I just can't figure out why the radio isn't . . ." She trailed off, scowling at the machine. "Here's a dry spot," she added. "Let's get you off this raft. Come on, Roger, you can do a little for yourself. One—two—three—there you go."

Between Ollie and Ms. Zintner, they got Mr. Adler to stand up and walk a few steps to a tall dry rock. "Here," Coco's mom said. "Sit down, Roger—you need to be still—*no*—" Mr. Adler was trying to get up, making incoherent noises. "You'll only make it worse, moving around."

Ollie retucked the emergency blanket around her dad. His hand had gone black, nearly to the wrist.

We have to get off this island, Brian thought.

But there was a *lake monster*—between them and everything else. Rescuers and hospitals. The whole world. Phil was still standing rigid, staring at the water.

Coco glanced up at the sky and then pulled out her phone. Made a face at whatever she saw.

Brian could guess what she'd seen: NO SERVICE.

"It's nearly five," she said, coming over to Brian. "When does it get dark?"

"Seven thirty?" said Brian. "I think. Somewhere in there." He tapped his lips with his finger. *STOP*, that was the acronym when you were in trouble.

Stop. Think. Observe. Plan. "We should figure out what we're going to do."

"Yeah," said Coco. She was frowning. "Is a lake monster *supernatural*? Or is it more like a strange animal? If it is supernatural, is it smart? Can it plan and think? Is it just gonna give up? Brian—" She bent her head closer, whispering. "Is this what the smiling man meant? A black spot—a death? Or are we all supposed to die here?"

Brian shuddered. "Mr. Dimmonds died," he said. Involuntarily, they both looked at Mr. Adler, sitting there hunched, holding his wrist with his good hand, his face an awful color. "Don't say anything about death to Ollie right now," added Brian.

Coco shook her head. "Ollie's thinking about it already," she said. Ollie's face looked pinched and afraid. Brian supposed his did as well. They all loved Mr. Adler.

The sun was still shining, but they were on the east side of the island, and the sun would set to the west. Pretty soon the light would go behind the dome-shaped rock over their heads, and they'd be in shadow. A long, cold breeze riffled the still water and Coco's straggling pinkish hair. Coco shivered. Brian shivered too. None of them were completely dry, what with the sloshing on the *Cassie* and the flying spray from the paddles as they raced toward shore.

Brian wished that they hadn't lost their bags, with their warm, dry jackets and hats. It was going to be freezing once the sun went away.

But hopefully, Brian thought, *we'll be off this island before dark.*

He knew they couldn't count on it, though.

Mr. Adler said, "Any sign of a boat?" His mouth was clenched down to a small, thin line.

"No, Dad," said Ollie. "But we're using the radio. I'm sure one will come soon." Ollie's splashed hair was curling and wet under her purple beanie. The first aid kit lay open beside her, as though Ollie had rummaged through it in sudden desperation.

Ms. Zintner was swearing at the radio. Coco was watching Brian. *Trusting* him. "At least you know about outdoor stuff," Coco said.

Brian took a deep breath. He had trusted Coco that winter, when she'd outsmarted the smiling man. She trusted him now to outsmart this cold, bare island. Brian tried to make his voice sound confident. He addressed the whole group. "Hey, guys? Um, question. Apart from Ollie's dad, is anyone else hurt?"

Confused silence as four pairs of eyes turned his

way. Brian had to repeat himself. Ollie spoke first. "I—no," she said. "I'm okay."

"I am too," said Coco.

"So am I," said Coco's mom. "Although I'm not sure—"

"Phil?" said Brian.

Phil looked up. "It doesn't matter. It's coming back," he said. "It's coming back for us. It hates us. Maybe that was its baby, the little snake I caught. It hates us."

Firmly Brian said, "Phil, come on. We need you with us. Come over here for a sec."

"Phil, your hand is bleeding," said Coco.

Phil looked down dully. Brian noticed it too: a spatter of little cuts. Brian said, "We should disinfect those."

"Why?" said Phil hollowly. "If we're just going to be eaten."

Coco said sharply, "Phil. It's a *lake* animal. It swims. How would it get on shore? Come on."

"Dunno," said Phil. But after a minute, he stopped staring at the lake and let Brian help him wrap up his hand.

"We only have a few hours until dark," said Brian. "We need to get ready. First, Ms. Zintner, does the radio work at all?"

"No," said Coco's mom in frustration. She glared down at it. The tip of her nose was red. "It's like, I can't find anything wrong with it. Except that it doesn't work. And I've been *trying* . . ."

Coco gave Brian one quick, meaningful glance. Brian didn't have to ask to know what she was thinking. They'd gone through a misty squall, they were on an uncharted island, and nothing worked.

And the smiling man was involved somehow.

It was definitely going to take more than a radio to get them home.

"All right," said Brian, and took a deep breath. "Well, we need a fire. That's the first thing. Someone out on the lake might see the smoke. And even if—" He swallowed. "*If* no one comes quick, then we're going to want a fire tonight. To stay warm, to dry off. We don't have enough clothes or blankets. Coco, are there emergency matches in the kit?"

Coco knelt to look. After a moment's digging, she held them up. Brian put them in his pocket.

"What about iodine tablets?" said Brian, and when Coco looked a little puzzled, he added, "For purifying water."

Coco, frowning, poked through the kit again. This time she held up a bottle.

"There's another bottle in there too," put in Phil. "A big one. Collapsible. To hold water." His voice was small, but at least he was listening now. The shadows stretched out from the forest toward them, like tentacles.

"Here," said Coco. "Found it."

"Okay," said Brian. "We need firewood. As much as we can get. Someone will see it pretty quick, I'm sure. Camping without a permit is illegal. Someone will come investigate a fire." He wasn't sure that was true. But it sounded encouraging.

Ms. Zintner managed a smile. "You're good at this, Brian," she said. "Can you boys go and get firewood? I'll keep trying to get the radio working. I might have to pull it apart to see what's wrong."

"Mom's good with machines," Coco said, and smiled, a little wobbly, at her mom. "She fixes the car and everything."

Brian didn't think it was a technical problem that was keeping the radio from working, and he could tell that Coco didn't think so either. But there wasn't really any point in saying that. He couldn't see Ollie's face at all. Just the top of her dark head as she bent over her dad.

"Ollie," said Coco softly, kneeling down by her friend. "Does your watch say anything?"

Ollie shrugged. She didn't look up. "It started a countdown," she said. "For—for five hours from now."

"That's good," said Brian. "We've got some time, then. Any idea what it's for?"

Ollie shook her head.

Brian glanced up. There were gray clouds gathering over the mountains in the distance.

I can do this, Brian told himself. *Last time, in the haunted lodge, I couldn't do anything. But I know about survival stuff. I can do this. I can keep everyone safe.*

"Well, we need firewood, no matter what," said Brian. "You with me, Phil?"

Phil nodded once, still looking lost.

"I'll go too," said Coco. She didn't like forests, Brian knew. They scared her. But Coco was really brave. Because a lot of things scared her, and she did what she thought was best anyway. "I can—" Her voice cracked. "I can help with the firewood. I think I'll do more good that way."

"Okay, hon," said her mother doubtfully. "But don't get lost, all right?"

"'Kay," said Coco.

"I'm staying here to take care of my dad," said Ollie. "I'll fill up the water bottle and put in the iodine tablets." She was digging into the emergency kit again as she spoke. "Hey—what's this?" she said.

"A smoke signal!" Brian said. "It'll make a lot of bright orange smoke. *Someone* is bound to see it!" Gingerly, he unscrewed the top of the smoke signal and put it on the ground. Instantly an enormous plume of brilliant orange smoke leapt up, hissing.

As soon as he saw it, Brian felt better. *If there's anyone around, they'll see it,* he thought. *It's huge.*

But only if there's anyone around, whispered another part of his brain. He ignored that part. "All right," said Brian. "Awesome. Now, how about that firewood? Let's go. Um, Ollie, Ms. Zintner? If a boat comes, just blow the whistle. And if not, we'll have a cozy fire to sit by until it *does* get here."

Brian headed for the woods, followed by Phil and Coco.

But Brian froze when he heard a hiss. A crackling noise, like static.

"Hey," said Coco's mom. "Hey—that's the radio!" She jumped over. "They must be broadcasting—have seen the smoke. Hello? Hello. Mayday, Mayday, request immediate assistance . . ."

No answer. Just the crackling. They all fell silent, listening. Brian frowned. There was the crackle of static, sure. But under that noise, it sounded like . . . breathing?

"Hello?" said Ms. Zintner again. "We were passengers on the *Cassandra*, out of Burlington, requesting immediate . . ."

"Where are you?" breathed a voice on the radio.

"I'm sorry?" said Ms. Zintner. "This is—" She stopped, because Coco had taken her arm very suddenly.

"Bill?" whispered the radio. *"Bill, are you there? I'm waiting for you, Billy . . . We're all waiting."*

"Beg pardon?" said Ms. Zintner.

"Leave," whispered the radio. Static drowned the next words, and then, *". . . never get off."*

"Who is this?" demanded Ms. Zintner sternly. "Are you on the island?"

There was only the sound of breathing, crackling over the radio. Then, *"Yes,"* whispered the radio. *"Forever forever forever . . ."* The voice faded away.

Brian took a breath to say something, although he didn't know what.

Then there was a sudden, enormously loud burst of static. *"Listen to the chimes!"* it roared, loud enough to make them all jump back. *"She sees in the dark,"* it whispered, almost too softly to hear. And then the radio cut out once more. The machine was silent.

"Well," said Ms. Zintner, after a pause. She was pale. "I guess there must be people on this island—some

97

awful practical jokers. But at least they're somewhere. Maybe, now that they've had their joke, we can—"

"I don't think it was a joke, Mom," Coco said.

"We need to make a fire," added Brian, trying for calm. There was no boat at all visible on the water, despite the smoke signal still spewing orange into the sky.

"Yeah," said Ollie, jaw set. "We really do." She glanced at her watch.

"Anything?" he asked her. Ollie, frowning, held it up so that Brian could see the screen. TELL, it said, flashing. Then it went back to the countdown. 4:56:53.

Brian didn't get it. "Tell what?" he said.

Ollie just shrugged, not quite meeting his eyes. "No idea," she said.

"Well," Brian said, "we'll just get some firewood, then. Ollie—" He looked from the radio, to her watch, and back to her face. "If you need us, we'll come running."

She nodded, not speaking.

He picked up one of the emergency whistles from the kit and handed it to Coco. "You're the most likely to get lost," he told her, and Coco didn't argue. She looked scared.

Brian glanced back at Ollie, just before he went into the woods. She was staring down at her watch.

Brian had the strangest feeling. As though Ollie knew perfectly well what her watch was trying to say.

As though she knew, but she hadn't told them.

That was ridiculous, he reminded himself. Ollie trusted them. They were her friends.

9

THE FOREST WAS thick, and all sound seemed muffled when they passed the first pine trees and the lake dropped out of sight behind them. Fresh growth capped the winter-dark needles of the spruce trees, and Brian snagged some of the spruce tips and stuffed them in his mouth. Coco watched him doubtfully.

"Are those—good to eat?" she asked.

"Yup," said Brian. "Well, they aren't White Rock Pizza, but they're okay. Piney. They have vitamin C, I think?" Coco tried one herself, made a face, chewing. He grinned at her and ate another handful.

The space under the trees was chilly, as though the pines had enclosed the remains of winter, safe under their branches. Here and there, the snow lay in patches, and the mud was glassy smooth and deep. They all slipped and slid in it. No birds sang. Brian saw, with annoyance, that a lot of the deadfall was damp. It would be harder to make a fire. But he bent down anyway and started picking up sticks.

Coco came up beside him. "What do you think it meant—*listen to the chimes?*" she asked.

"I don't know," he said.

Phil said, breaking a dry branch over his knee, "That radio was just a practical joke. Just a stupid joke. Someone on the island is playing *jokes*. We just need to find that person and tell them that—that this is serious and—"

"Phil," said Coco, rounding on him. "What happened to us all, in October?"

That was obviously a question Phil hadn't expected. He straightened, dropping the stick. "I—amnesia?"

"It's not amnesia if you *remember*," said Coco implacably. "Do you remember?"

Phil flushed bright red, then white, then muttered, "You wouldn't believe me. When I tried to tell—Mom just took me to a counselor. Maybe I did imagine it."

"The scarecrows?" said Coco, her eyes fierce. "When you and the rest of the sixth grade were *kidnapped off the bus and turned into scarecrows?* Do you remember that?"

Phil's mouth opened. Then closed again. He whispered, "No. No way."

"Yes way," Brian broke in. "Or was there not a lake monster? Are you going to say we *imagined* that too? The world is full of weird stuff, and we—"

But Phil was obviously not listening to him. "You *knew* what happened?" he breathed. "In October? All this time? You knew the scarecrows were real? You knew that all of it was real? *All three of you knew?*"

Brian nodded.

Phil punched him. It wasn't a very good punch, more a shove, but it took Brian by surprise and dropped him, painfully, onto the rocks and roots of the forest floor. "Hey!" yelped Coco. "Hey, cool it!"

Phil glared at them both. "I thought I was crazy," he said. "Brian, I thought you wouldn't talk to me because you *knew I was crazy.* I thought I was *all by myself.* Why do you think I even talked to—to your smiling man, let him give me his stupid fishing lure? Because he was nice to me. He *believed* me. Not just some stupid 'I believe that you believe' thing, like the shrink. *He actually believed me.* He *listened* to me." And then, Phil burst into tears.

Brian got to his feet, brushing dirt from his palms. He thought of how alone and afraid they'd felt that winter. But—he and Ollie and Coco hadn't really been alone. Not like Phil. They'd had each other. Phil hadn't had anyone. He'd just been stuck alone with nightmares and a sketchbook, maybe waiting for a scarecrow to come and scratch the glass of his window. And all the while, people he trusted were telling him that what he remembered hadn't happened.

"Phil," said Coco, in a new voice. "We're really sorry."

"Yeah," said Brian. "Phil—I didn't know."

Phil scrubbed over his eyes with one hand. "You didn't know because you didn't ask. You didn't care," he said furiously. "You just cared about each other."

"No," said Brian. "I—we wanted to keep everyone safe. We figured that—if people didn't remember, then they were better off not knowing."

"I remembered," said Phil. "And I wasn't better off. I thought we were friends, Brian."

"I'm sorry," said Brian. "We should have—should have tried harder."

Coco wasn't even giving Brian an I-told-you-so look. She was frowning at Phil in concern. Phil glanced up and saw it. "Why are you even nice to me?" Phil demanded of Coco. "I've never been nice to you."

Coco said, after a pause to think, "Well, I was mad in October. You made me cry. But then you got kidnapped and turned into a scarecrow. And also, if you hadn't been mean, Ollie wouldn't have tried to rescue me, I wouldn't have left the bus with her, and I'd probably be a scarecrow myself now. Plus you apologized on the boat. So I'm not mad anymore. Are you going to be mean again?"

"Um, no," said Phil, looking bemused. He wiped his wet eyes. "No, I'm not. I—uh—I'm sorry I made you cry."

"Are you going to make anyone else cry?"

He shook his head. "Not on purpose."

"Well, then," said Coco. "We're stuck on a creepy island, this isn't really a good time to hold grudges anyway. Let's grab firewood."

"Yeah," said Brian. "We need to hurry." The wind was picking up. Coco had vivid patches of color on her nose and cheeks. It would only get colder.

"So," said Phil in a subdued voice, starting to collect sticks. "If the scarecrows were real, and the lake monster was real . . ."

"Then whoever was on the radio just now might not have been joking," Brian finished for him. "Ghosts are real too." He was breaking up a dead tree branch over his knee as he spoke, thinking of other ghosts, other places where the ordinary rules didn't apply. He was also thinking that getting off this island was definitely not going to be as simple as signaling for rescue.

They started collecting wood in earnest. There was a decent amount of deadfall. The three of them spread out, picking up sticks as quick as they could. Brian had brought the rope from the lifeboat to tie the sticks up into bundles.

When they had gathered enough for the first bundle, Brian hauled it back toward the lake, leaving the others gathering more, a little ways into the forest. He got back down to the water and found Ms. Zintner poking at the radio.

"Anything?" Brian asked her, not sure if he meant anything creepy or anything encouraging. Anything at all, probably.

Ms. Zintner just shook her head. Her blond hair stuck to her neck. She was kneeling on pebbles, glaring at the radio lying on the ground in front of her. "Why does technology never work when you need it to?"

Ollie was sitting with her dad, their backs against the same flat rock. He had his eyes closed. Ollie had huddled up as close to him as she could, with the foil blanket around them both. She'd put her purple beanie on his head. She glanced at her watch, then back to the lake. The shadows flickered, the sun moved, the temperature was dropping.

"Anything new?" Brian asked.

Ollie shook her head, still staring at the water. But then she turned to look at Brian, and he saw her face was pale and scared. He'd never seen her looking so scared, even when there were scarecrows getting ready to grab them.

"Dad's cold," she said. "He's *really* cold."

Ms. Zintner swore at the radio, then abandoned it and came over to them. "I'll start a fire," she said.

"It's okay," said Brian. "I'll do it, Ms. Zintner. I'm good at fires." He dropped his bundle of sticks and got to work. He *was* good at fires. He couldn't help but notice that the big orange smoke signal had died down, but there was no sign of anyone on the water.

"How you doing, Dad?" said Ollie.

Mr. Adler's eyes slowly opened. His lips were cracking. "Been better," he said. "How's that rescue coming?"

"Not too good," said Ollie. "No one's seen us." She swallowed. "Dad—we might have to spend the night. On this island."

"That's okay," said her dad, his eyes drifting shut once more. "S'okay—it'll be like camping . . . just like camping."

"Dad?" said Ollie, her voice going shrill. "Dad!"

Ms. Zintner put her fingers up to Mr. Adler's neck, checking his pulse. "Just asleep, Ollie," she said. But she looked frightened. Almost as frightened as Ollie. Ollie glanced down at her watch again, her shoulders hunched small.

Brian was struck again by the thought that Ollie knew more than she was saying about that countdown. But he didn't want to press her. Not when he needed to hurry back into the trees to get them more firewood. Not when Ollie looked so frightened. He wished he could do something else for her. He wished he had a snake-venom cure or a boat-calling spell. But all he could do was make a fire and wait.

Brian struck a match and ignited the handful of pine needles he'd grabbed for kindling. The pine needles caught fire fast. Brian breathed on the tiny flames, trying to make them catch. When he had a tidy fire going, he said, "I'm going back to help the others with the wood. Don't let the fire go out, okay?"

"Thanks, Brian," said Ms. Zintner, smiling at him.

As Brian trudged toward the woods, he glanced back. Ms. Zintner had put her arm around Ollie, and he could see, as she turned her head into the light, the shine of tears on Ollie's face.

10

IN THE WOODS, the shadows were getting longer and longer. It would be dark soon.

"Coco!" Brian called when he got into the trees. "Phil?"

Silence met his call. He felt a little cold finger of dread creep down his spine. A few minutes ago, they'd been stepping on branches and calling to each other in the gathering shadows.

"Hey!" he bellowed. "Coco! Phil!"

Still nothing. He started to push through the woods, calling their names. The silence seemed to drill into his head. Where were they?

He stopped to listen again. This time he heard Phil shout. Brian hurried toward the sound. The hair on the back of his neck was prickling. They'd left the lake monster in the water, along with the *Cassandra*. But—who had put the carving on the tree? Who had been on the radio? What was waiting for them, on this still, silent island?

"Phil!" he yelled. "Phil, where are you?"

"Here!" yelled Phil.

Brian angled again in the direction of Phil's voice, pushing through the branches. There weren't any paths, just different thicknesses of undergrowth.

Brian almost plowed into Phil; he hadn't been that far away. The dense trees muffled and turned sounds.

Phil was standing in the middle of a clearing, frowning down at the ground. Brian followed his line of vision. What was that? It looked like trash. A giant heap of it, like a tarp or plastic, a clear grayish-white. Winding around the trees.

Brian's first thought was relief. "Trash!" he said. He'd never in his whole life felt relieved to find trash out in nature before, but there was a first time for everything. Trash meant people; trash meant other people came to this island. Trash meant they weren't trapped.

Then he paused. It looked like trash, but it looked like something else too. Something familiar, but not—not so big.

He stared hard at that pile of trash.

"No," he said. With a hand that shook more than he wanted, he reached out and touched it. A little damp. Papery. Almost translucent, when he put his hand close. Just like . . .

Phil whispered, "It's a snakeskin."

It *was* a snakeskin. Now that Brian's eyes had adjusted to the size—and *how* could a snake be that big?—it was obvious.

"It comes on land," said Phil. "Just like—like a regular water snake. It comes on land."

Brian didn't say anything right away, but his heart had started to race. His chest felt tight; his breath came short.

Phil went on. "Water snakes are crepuscular," he said. Phil had always been good at science class. "That means they hunt at dawn and dusk. And sometimes—sometimes they hunt at night."

Brian whipped around, shouting, "Coco! Coco!"

No answer.

A sick, cold fear filled Brian's head.

"When did you last see her?" he demanded of Phil.

"Dunno," said Phil. He was looking scared too. "Ten minutes ago? I heard her—she makes a lot of noise—but then I saw this, and I stopped listening . . . Maybe she went back toward the beach?"

Brian turned and pushed through the trees, back in the direction of the water. He was furious at himself for letting them all split up. *Didn't you learn that this winter?* his angry inner voice demanded. *You can't split up! Splitting up means your friends get lost and bad things happen.*

And Coco was smart, but she was no good in forests. "Coco!" he shouted. *"Coco!"*

No answer. Only the silence of the trees.

And then Brian heard a sound that relieved him and froze him cold with terror at the same time. A long, shrill whistle. The sound of the emergency whistle that Coco was carrying.

Brian started to bolt toward the sound. Phil seized him by the arm and brought him up short. "Hey, buddy. You're not thinking. What if the snake *is* here and it's—hunting? Coco hasn't been eaten yet, or she wouldn't have blown the whistle. *We* don't want to get eaten either."

Brian yanked his arm out of Phil's grip, straining his ears, listening. He wanted to snap at Phil, but he bit his tongue and tried to make himself think properly. Phil wasn't saying that they should run away or anything. He was just saying that they should be careful. Which wasn't bad advice. Besides, Phil looked terrified—understandably—since he'd seen the snake *snatch his uncle*, and he was still there, not running in blind panic. If Phil could manage not to panic, then Brian could too.

Brian took a deep breath. "'Kay," he said. "Okay. We'll be careful. Do you—do you remember anything about *how* water snakes hunt?"

Phil frowned. "Well, crepuscular. They hunt at dawn and dusk. And um . . . that's about it, really. Sorry." He shook his head. "Let's be really careful," he said. "Keep an eye out." He picked up a thick tree branch, the most solid of the pieces of firewood they'd just gathered.

Brian grabbed a stick too. "Let's go," he said.

They began moving in the direction of Coco's whistle. The light was fading now.

Another whistle tore through the trees. They hurried as fast as they dared toward the sound, peering in all directions, holding tight to their sticks.

Suddenly Brian grabbed Phil's arm. "What's that?" he said.

Phil stopped. He was sweating all over his face, even though it was chilly. A few hundred yards farther in, there was a fishhook hanging from a tree branch. A big, rusted fishhook.

"There too," said Phil, pointing in another direction. Brian followed his friend's finger. Another fishhook. And another. The trees, he realized, were full of fishhooks. Dangling fishhooks. Big and small. Old and rusted.

They'd been hung from tree branches on short lengths of rope. In some places, Brian saw that the ropes had worn thin with rot and the fishhooks lay on the ground, brown with rust and hard to see.

"At least we know people come here?" breathed Phil. "Or else who hung these up?"

The fishhooks swayed softly in the breeze, needle-sharp at the tips. They chimed together, like they were alive and talking. Brian didn't like it.

"The radio," Brian said, remembering. *"Listen to the chimes . . ."*

"But why?" said Phil. "Who would hang up all those fishhooks?"

"I don't know," said Brian. He was listening hard. Coco hadn't whistled again. Which way?

Why would someone hang fishhooks from trees?

He heard a chiming off to their right as more fishhooks swung together.

"Brian," whispered Phil. "Brian, I thought I saw something moving."

"Do you think it was Coco?" Brian whispered back.

Phil was shaking. "I—I don't know . . ."

Just then, Coco herself popped out from between the trees. Phil and Brian both yelped.

Brian sucked in a relieved breath. "Geez, you scared us." He listened for the fishhooks again, but they'd gone still.

"Sorry," said Coco. "I didn't mean to." She looked excited.

"What is it?" said Brian. He shot a suspicious look around. But now nothing moved.

"Here," said Coco, with the air of a successful magician. She disappeared between two trees. Brian and Phil, still nervous, followed.

Coco scraped through some bushes and pointed. What was that? A boulder? No, a weathered building, nearly hidden in the trees and the late-afternoon shadows. Coco looked proud of herself. "A cabin," she said. "That's why I whistled. If I actually tried to go get you, I'd have never found this place again."

"Coco, this is amazing, but we're not safe. We need to get back to the beach," said Brian. Phil was still shooting the forest nervous glances. Brian told Coco about the snakeskin.

She shot a scared look out into the trees. "What if we go and get the others and bring them back here?" she asked. "Safer than being out in the open, if—if the snake is around. Maybe warmer too."

"Yeah, but whose cabin is this?" asked Brian. The grayish, weathered cabin door hung slightly crooked.

"I don't know," said Coco. "But—I mean—does it matter? Who would mind us using their cabin? We're *shipwrecked*."

"Truth," said Brian. He stared again into the silent trees. All the fishhooks hung still. They were probably okay. Just because they'd found a snakeskin didn't mean the snake came onshore *often*. It didn't mean it was hunting. It had probably tired itself out sinking the *Cassandra*.

But he still hesitated at the threshold of the cabin. They didn't have a good history with old, weird buildings. "Coco, have you been inside?"

She shook her head. "I saw it and whistled and then waited for you. I didn't think it was safe to go in alone." Coco also seemed to be thinking about their history with old buildings. She added, "But pretty much any building is better than spending the night out, right? It's going to be awfully cold, and Mr. Adler will need to be warm. And this cabin looks abandoned."

"Who cares if it's abandoned or not?" asked Phil. "Better if it's not! Anyone living here would have a boat, remember? Come *on*, let's check it out!"

He pushed through the door before Coco or Brian could say anything else. After another moment's indecision, Brian and Coco followed.

The inside of the cabin was dim. Almost dark. There were no windows, just the narrow, crooked door. The walls were strangely thick, reinforced with pieces of wood nailed on everywhere. And why were there no windows?

"Hang on," said Brian, and dug out the emergency flashlight that he'd stashed in a pocket. He shined it around the room.

Phil screamed.

Coco didn't, but he heard her breath catch in a small, horrified gasp. There was a skeleton on the bed.

Or a skull at least. Probably more than just a skull, Brian thought, swallowing hard. The rest of the skeleton was covered by a blanket, except for one arm. The skull lay on a moldy pillow, fallen sideways, turned toward them. The empty sockets seemed to stare. Its yellowed teeth smiled. Its arm bones lay along the grimy wool blanket. On its chest, under one bony hand, lay a black book bound in leather.

"Oh geez," Phil whispered.

"Never mind. Let's get out of here," Coco whispered.

"Hang on," said Brian. He turned his light onto the rest of the room—anything to look away from the skeleton's empty eye sockets—and caught sight of a pile of firewood, bone dry, neatly cut and stacked, lying near the door. Not sticks. Logs. Logs that would keep a fire going all night. That would keep Mr. Adler warm until help arrived.

"We should take the wood with us," he said.

"No way!" said Phil. He stood on the threshold, as though he were on the edge of bolting. "This doesn't belong to us. It's—it belongs to whoever died here. That guy." He didn't look at the skeleton. Besides the bed and its occupant, there wasn't much in the cabin at all. Some old, rotten fabric, some bits of rusty metal, a coil of old rope. Leaves and dust blown in from the crooked front door.

Coco was staring at the bed as though she couldn't look away. But she took a deep breath and said, "Phil, Brian's right. The wood isn't helping—whoever that is on the bed—but it might help us."

Phil didn't say anything. Brian said, "Okay, okay, Phil—maybe just keep watch? I'll use this rope and make up some bundles of firewood. We'll be out of here in a sec. We don't need to spend the night. It might be hard for Mr. Adler to move, anyway . . ."

Talking, half babbling, anything to keep his mind off the shadows and the dust and the bones in the small musty bed, Brian bent and began to separate the wood into piles.

While Brian worked, Coco drifted nearer to the bed. Phil said, "What are you doing?"

Coco said, "He's probably lonely. Was." She looked down at the skeleton, and she seemed more sad than scared. "I wonder what happened to him?" She reached out to touch the book atop the blanket. Gently, she picked it up.

Brian said, "Coco, I'm not sure that's a good idea."

"Me either," said Coco. "But I think this is some kind of journal. Maybe we'll find out what happened to him. Maybe we can find out who he was and find his family and get him buried properly!"

"I'd worry more about getting off this island ourselves than about what comes after that," said Brian, tying a neat knot on the second bundle. He started to make a third, using his pocketknife to cut the rope.

"Fair," said Coco. "But still." She slipped the black book into her big jacket pocket. "I'll bring it back," she said gently to the bones. "And maybe I'll find your people, okay?"

Brian shivered. A thick, endless silence seemed to lie on the cabin. He thought about the bones lying here for—how long?—through rain, snow, heat . . .

He didn't want to think about it. They needed to get Mr. Adler to a hospital. That was the most important thing. Not old cabins and old secrets.

"Here," he said, handing Coco a bundle of firewood. "Phil, we're going."

"Hang on," said Phil. He'd gone back to the cabin door. "Did you hear that?"

"What?" said Brian, trying to hand off the second bundle of firewood.

"*Listen,*" said Phil.

They all stopped. They all listened. "I don't hear anything," said Brian, after a moment. "Phil, we need to get back. Let's go back and get the others—" He fell silent. He'd heard it too.

Someone was whistling. Ordinary, uncomplicated whistling, the way Mr. Adler liked to do when he was baking. But this wasn't Mr. Adler. After a minute, the whistling turned, full-voiced, into song, and it was a deep voice that Brian had never heard in his life.

"*She started with his hair,*" sang the strange voice. "*And then she ate his eyes.*"

There was the swish of footsteps in leaf mold. Coming closer.

"And as he sang his last sweet tune / She—"

The song broke off. "What's this?" said the voice. "What's this here? Footprints? Footprints?" The voice was a man's: deep and rather cracked, as though the speaker had a cold or had screamed himself hoarse. "Tommy, is that you?"

Phil had his mouth open, as though to call to the unknown singer. Coco grabbed his arm, pinching. Brian thought she was right. If they were behind the mist, if they were in another of the smiling man's games, you couldn't trust anyone. They'd trusted a ghost once and nearly lost Ollie because of it.

"Allen?" asked the voice, sounding eager. "Jimmy?"

The voice was coming closer. The cabin was small. The cabin only had one door, and no windows. The footsteps were right outside. There was nowhere to go.

And now there wasn't time. The door flew open and slammed against the far wall, with a scream of hinges and a shower of dust. A stranger stood in the gap. He had a rusty axe slung over one shoulder.

11

FOR A SECOND, everyone just stared. Then—"Who are you?" demanded the stranger, bristling at them. "Thieves? Trying to wake up Tommy, are ye? Well, he won't wake. I tried already." He glared at the bones with bloodshot dark eyes. "Ungrateful sod. After how long I've protected him."

Brian, staring at the man in the doorway, found himself terribly conscious of the shadowy gaze of the skull at his back.

The stranger had enormous, bushy eyebrows that dominated a face the color of modeling clay. One shoulder was a lot higher than the other, and he was *huge*—his head thrust forward and the back of his neck brushed the lintel of the door. His beard poured down his chest in a series of bristles. Brian licked his lips. "I'm Brian," he said. "This is Phil, and that's Coco. Our boat sank."

"Sank, did it?" said the man, looking from one of them to the other. "Marooned, are you? Me an' Tommy know all about that." He gave the skull a conspiratorial grin that faded quickly. "Or did. Tommy won't talk to me anymore—"

"No!" said Phil. "Not marooned. We're waiting for a boat. A boat's coming to pick us up."

"And you thought you'd wait here, did you? Thought you'd take me 'n' Tommy's cabin for yerself, did yer?" He pulled the axe down off his shoulder and hefted it.

"No!" chimed in Coco, almost yelping. "No, we just—saw it and wondered who lived here. We wondered if you could help us?" Her voice had started off confident but faded as she kept talking. The stranger's eyes were wild in his clay-colored face.

"Help you?" said the stranger. "Want me to axe you, do yer? Want me to axe you and leave you in here with Tommy, so that you don't have to wait? Wait like I'm waiting? Wait for the thing in the woods?" He shuddered. Then his face softened. "Poor kids. I'll axe you if you like." He raised the axe. "No bed, of course, but ye can have the floor. Tommy won't mind. Hold still . . ."

Coco yelped, backing up. "*Axe* us? No—we don't want—that."

The axe was lowered. A frown creased the stranger's face. "Well, sure," he said. "Better the axe than what's coming for you."

"What's coming for us?" whispered Brian.

The stranger laughed at him. High, wild, shrill laughter spilled out of his mouth, rising and rising, awful, not sane. His teeth were ground down, rotted and gapped; the inside of his mouth was black. "Oh, you'll find out," he said. "I got my axe ready for any-one who wants it. You're not getting off, you see. Not nohow, not never. I never got off, don'tcha see. I got the boys off, but not me. Can't leave while she's still here. Gotta get her. Gotta do it for Tommy . . ."

"Who?" demanded Phil. "And you're wrong. We're totally getting off this island. We—"

He was interrupted by Coco shouting, "Shut up shut up shut *up!*"

When Brian and Phil swung round to look at her, she said, "I think I heard something. Out there in the trees."

"Poor kids," muttered the man. "Poor kids, they don't know any better. Not fair to give them a choice when they don't know any better." He raised his axe again and advanced into the room. His expression was horribly caring.

Brian, cold with terror, did the only thing he could think to do. He snatched up the skull. "Axe any of us, and Tommy gets it," he said.

The man froze again. "Now," he said, "you wouldn't hurt Tommy, would you? Understand, it's for your own good—"

Brian threw the skull. The stranger dropped his axe to catch it, cradling it in his two huge hands, and in the moment he was distracted, Brian snatched up the axe in one hand and his bundle of wood in the other.

"Coco, come *on!*" he bellowed, and the three of them dashed into the trees. Faintly, Brian heard the sound of the man, weeping, in the cabin at their backs.

"Tommy," he wailed. "Tommeeeee! Why'd you hurt him? Why'd you hurt him!"

The sound was swallowed by the muffling trees.

They could not go as fast as they wanted to. The ground was slick with mud. The forest was so still that Brian could hear the thud of every footstep, the sound of everyone's breathing.

The ground sloped down toward the beach. They trotted as fast as they dared, in single file, heaving their bundles of wood. Brian and Phil had managed to snag theirs; Coco hadn't. But it was all right, Brian thought. They had enough for the night.

Beyond that . . . well, he didn't know.

"Wait," said Coco, panting, at the same moment as Phil whispered, "I thought I saw something." They all stopped, and they peered, and they listened. Brian didn't see or hear anything.

"What did it look like?" he whispered. "Was it—do you think it was the axe man again?"

Phil shook his head, squinting.

Then Brian heard something. A faint chiming. The fishhooks were crashing into each other. Like they were a beaded curtain and someone had just run through it.

"Nothing," said Coco. She sounded relieved. They kept on going toward the beach.

Silence under the trees.

Then they heard the fishhooks again. This time, the chiming was a little closer.

Brian strained his eyes through the gathering dark. Didn't see anything.

"Trees," muttered Phil. "What is it about trees? I feel like there's something important . . ." There was sweat on Brian's palms, on the back of his neck, even though it was cold already and getting colder.

A chiming off to the right. Closer.

"Water snakes like trees," murmured Phil, as though he were reciting from memory. "They sometimes come out of the water and perch in trees to . . ."

He paused.

"To . . ."

A chime from the fishhooks in the trees right behind them.

"Hunt," Phil whispered.

Brian turned around. His mouth went dry as dust. Ten feet of snake had unwound itself from a branch overhead. Its open cotton-pink mouth was four feet away, jammed with teeth.

Phil screamed, and Coco gasped. *"Run!"* bellowed Brian. All three of them bolted. Brian thought he heard the sound of the axe man laughing—or maybe he was screaming—somewhere in the dimness. Behind them the hooks clanged together. Brian risked a look back, saw the snake heaving its body from a branch, slowed down by three or four big fishhooks that had gotten jammed into its side. But fishhooks obviously weren't going to slow this thing down for long.

Brian didn't think they could outrun it. He was already pulling ahead of Phil and Coco. And it was only a matter of time before Coco . . .

Thud.

Coco had already tripped, slipping in the glassy mud. She hauled herself to her feet just as Brian whipped around to help her, but the snake had yanked free of the fishhooks and was gaining on them. It wasn't bothering to be sneaky now. It was just coming like a wave, its body sliding across the ground in wild loops, faster than they could run, its eyes white and cloudy, its toothy mouth open.

"Coco, come *on!*" he cried, and they took off again.

A stitch was forming in Brian's side. He'd never run so hard in his life. Phil was sobbing for breath just behind him. Coco was running along gamely, stumbling on roots, but slow, too slow. Brian's brain raced like a gerbil in a cage. They could climb a tree. But so could the snake.

Maybe, if they got high enough, they could get higher than the massive thing could reach?

What choice did they have?

"Coco!" he said. "We have to climb!" He saw Coco's eyes go wide with understanding. But Coco, being Coco, didn't say anything. She just, without a word, turned sideways, got a foot on the trunk of the nearest pine, and *jumped*, stretching up as high she could go. She snagged the lowest branch just as Phil came up, panting. Phil wasn't that good at climbing trees. Brian hastily knelt, cupping his hands.

"Phil," he said. "Put a foot in my hand and . . . *now!*" he snapped when Phil hesitated, looking between the tree and the oncoming lake monster.

Phil put a foot on Brian's interlaced fingers, and Brian heaved him upward with all his strength, giving his friend just enough height to grab the lowest branch of the tree. Coco caught his hands when he would have slipped and instructed, "Put your feet up! No, there, against the trunk!"

For a heart-stopping moment, Brian thought Phil was going to fall and that there wouldn't be time to try again. But Phil steadied, got his hands on a higher branch, and then he and Coco were just climbing frantically, while Brian jumped for the lowest branch himself, hooked his legs around it.

Coco was already ten feet above, pulling herself up like a gymnast through the branches. Phil was slower. Brian caught up. "Come on, Phil, faster!" he said.

He risked a glance down.

The snake was coming up like a silver river. Coco had picked a massive old tree, thankfully; otherwise, Brian was pretty sure a snake that could sink boats could just knock the tree down. But if they didn't get high enough, it could just heave its body straight up and pluck them out.

It was below the tree now and rearing its body high through the branches. Brian saw the fangs, glistening with venom, come close to Phil's ankle. Phil shrieked and scrabbled upward, and the snake fell back.

But then it tried to climb the tree. Up it went, wrapping the old trunk like a glittering, deadly vine.

The lower branches held under its enormous weight. Coco had already gone up as high as she dared; Brian had to stop at the branch below her; he weighed more than she did. Phil joined him, gasping. His hands were bleeding from the bark. They all stared down. Nowhere to go, and the snake was still climbing. Higher and higher it climbed. Brian saw tears leaking from Phil's stretched-wide eyes. What could they do? Throw something at it? How? He was clutching his branch with both hands, and there were no dead branches convenient . . .

Closer and closer the pink mouth came.

Suddenly, they heard a crack from somewhere below. Then another. There was a hiss. And then four more cracks came at once and the branches under the snake broke. It tumbled to the ground, hissing. Brian, shaking, his hands dripping sweat, feeling sick from the adrenaline, hoped it had been hurt.

It hadn't, though. It tried to nose its way back up the tree, must have realized its support branches were gone.

It'll leave now, Brian thought. *It'll realize it can't get up here, and it will go looking for something easier.*

Then his whole body went cold, for, of course, who could be easier than Ollie and her dad and Coco's mom, just sitting by the lake, totally unaware of the danger?

"Hey!" he yelled absurdly at the snake. "Hey, look up here! Look at us, you jerk! Hey!"

Now, when the snake wasn't five feet away, he was able to unpeel a hand from his branch, break off a pine cone, and hurl it down. He wished he hadn't dropped the axe. The pine cone bounced off the snake's nose.

"Brian," said Phil, sounding appalled. His voice was still shaking. "What are you doing?"

Coco had understood. "Mom," she whispered, still panting. "And Ollie. They don't know . . ."

But the snake—fortunately, or horribly—was showing no signs of leaving. It had coiled itself up around the tree. Brian could see one of its bulging filmy eyes turned up and watching them even though the light had begun to fail. Brian supposed that was what he wanted. But . . .

They were stuck in a tree. With a snake waiting for them to fall asleep. To fall.

To eat them.

And night was coming on. The air blew frigid off the water.

"This can't be good," said Phil. Coco and Brian didn't say anything at all.

12

THEY JUST CLUNG to their branches, catching their breaths, for a couple of minutes. Then Brian, trying to think, said, "Coco—can you see over the treetop? Can you see the beach?"

Coco stood up, balancing dangerously. "Yeah. I can see their fire. I hope that—Champ—is scared of fire." She bent an anxious face down toward them. "You don't think that Ollie and Mom heard me whistle, before?" she asked. "You don't think my mom would go into the woods after me?"

Brian thought she would if Coco was in danger. *His* mom certainly would. Aloud he said, trying to be reassuring, "I don't think she'd leave Ollie and her dad." That was maybe true. He hoped it was. It was getting darker under the trees. The snake had coiled up, watching them with flat old eyes, its tongue flicking in and out, a silver shadow among the gray ones at the base of the tree.

"Now what?" Phil said.

"Good question," said Coco.

Brian tried to think. Being stuck in a tree, breathless, wasn't really good for thinking. He was tired, he was cold, he was scared. He wished the snake would go away. But if it went away, Ollie and Mr. Adler and Coco's mom . . .

"Do either of you think the guy with the axe would help us?" asked Phil uncertainly.

"He offered to help us by *axing* us," said Coco. "Besides, Brian threw a skull at him." She shuddered. "And it sounded like the skull was his buddy. I'm pretty sure he won't help us."

"Sorry," said Brian. "I couldn't think of anything else."

"No, you saved us," said Coco. "It was just—awful. Do you think he was a ghost?"

"The axe man?" asked Phil, his voice going a little squeaky.

"Probably," said Brian. "He was wearing old-timey clothes, from what I could tell. And he had that—that grayish look. And he was really serious about one thing, about his friend Tommy. I feel like ghosts usually are really stuck on one thing . . ."

"Yeah," said Coco. "I wonder if Tommy's a ghost too. And if not, why not?"

"Ghosts?" said Phil.

"Um, yeah," said Brian. "Really long story. But you can trust us on this one."

"Right," said Phil. "Sure. Trust you." After Brian and Coco hadn't said anything for a few minutes, Phil added, "Why aren't you guys freaking out more? There's a *giant water snake* trying to eat us, we're stuck in a tree, and there was a guy just there who wanted to *axe* us, and you think he might be a ghost, and this is awful."

Brian and Coco looked at each other. "Not our first time?" offered Coco after a moment, a little helplessly.

Brian peered again down through the branches. It was already harder to make out the edges of the silvery creature in the gloom. What were they going to do?

"Okay," Phil said. "When we get out of this, you promise to tell me everything. No more secrets. I'm on the team now, right?" He was clearly trying to sound determined, but he mostly just sounded worried.

"Yeah," said Brian to Phil. "You're with us in the snake tree. On the team. No more secrets."

"Great," said Phil. "So I can ask again: now what?"

"I don't know," said Brian testily. "How am I supposed to know? You know more about snakes than I do."

"Dude, you know more about weird stuff than I do, so—"

"This isn't helping," interrupted Coco. She was lying flat on the branch above them, feet and hands hooked around the limb like a cat. "We have to figure out something *soon*. We can't let Ollie or my mom come into the woods to look for us."

"Right," said Brian. He thought. "Um, do you think it's scared of fire?"

His friends both looked at him doubtfully. "Why do you ask?" said Phil.

"Well, if fire scares it away," said Brian, "then Ollie and her dad and Coco's mom are pretty safe on the beach. Unless their fire goes out. And maybe," he added, feeling inspired, "we can light up some pine cones and drop them, and maybe drop a few of these fishhooks too. That would scare it maybe? Give us a chance to get away?"

"Pine cones?" Phil said. "It's built like—like a boat-sized snake!"

"What if we dropped them down its throat?" said Brian.

"But it only opens its mouth when it's mad or about to eat something . . ." Coco trailed off. "You can't be serious." She looked between Brian and Phil. "Right," she said. "You are serious. You want to make the snake mad."

Brian said, "Got a better idea?"

Neither of them did.

"Okay, If we need bait, then I'll be bait," Coco said, after Brian had outlined his plan. "I don't think pine cones will make it mad enough. What if I go down and get the firewood? I think Phil dropped his bundle pretty close to the tree. We could drop chunks of firewood on it. Or would the axe help? Didn't you grab the axe?" She squinted into the darkness.

"I dropped it," said Brian. "Running for our lives and all. Also climbing to the ground would be way too dangerous. Let's start just by throwing fishhooks. And burning pine cones." Their tree, like the others, had hooks tied into its branches. Someone's early warning system, Brian thought. What had happened to *them*? He hoped that the skeleton lying in the cabin hadn't put up the fishhooks. That wasn't a good sign for *their* chances.

Coco and Brian had begun clambering around the tree, passing his pocketknife between them and collecting some of the biggest fishhooks. The big ones were bigger than Coco's face.

Brian had put a few of the biggest hooks over his arm, trying not to poke himself. He was glad he wasn't afraid of heights. Coco was standing on the branch above them. "Coco, it was my idea," he called up to her. "I'll be bait."

"Don't be ridiculous," said Coco. "I'm way better at climbing than you, and I can't throw. Either I'm bait, or I don't help at all."

Phil gave her a puzzled look. Brian could understand why. No one at school saw Coco like this. In school, Coco was small and clumsy and kind of squeaky. She wasn't the best at PE or anything. She liked to draw. She liked things that sparkled. She tripped over her own feet a lot. She always looked a little like a flower fairy.

She still did now, but it was the less-nice kind of flower fairy. The kind that maybe lived in a toadstool and defended the forest from invaders. Her pinkish hair straggled down her back, and she pushed strands of it off her face. Her eyes were narrow, her sparkly sneakers confident on the branch.

Phil said, with an anxious croak, "If you guys are sure about this—*I'll* throw. If you light stuff on fire, Brian."

Brian bit his lip and then he nodded. Logically, it was the best division of tasks. Coco, who was the smallest and the best climber, would be bait. Brian, who was good at making fires, would light up the missiles. And Phil, who was the pitcher for the middle school baseball team, would do the throwing.

But he felt cold and sick and scared. It wasn't that great a plan. But what choice did they have? Coco climbed a few feet down. "Hey!" she yelled. "Hey, Lurky! Look up here!"

A huge filmy eye opened below them, shiny in the gloom. Brian stuck a rusted fishhook through a pine cone, getting ready to touch a flaming match to it and . . .

Somewhere in the woods, the axe man started singing. A new song this time. Brian turned his head involuntarily to listen.

"*But one man of her crew alive,*" sang the axe man. "*What put to sea with seventy-five . . .*"

The song faded into a giggle, high-pitched.

"Does he know we're here?" demanded Phil. "In the tree? And he's just . . . hanging around? Is he *making fun of us?*"

136

"I don't know," said Brian grimly. He lit his first pine cone and handed it to Phil to throw.

It fizzled up with flames, but when Phil hurled it down, the thing just bounced off of the creature's head, the fire already out, and the snake didn't even twitch. Brian caught the shine of its filmy, baleful eye still turned up to them, but its mouth wasn't open, and it wasn't mad. It was just . . . waiting. He thought a string of very bad words.

"Well," said Coco, "I think we need the firewood. I can see where you dropped them from here." Brian heard the quiver of breathless fear in her voice.

Phil said, "Coco, come on, the snake is right there! Look at what happened to Mr. Adler. Look at what happened to my uncle!"

Coco was scanning the ground below the tree. Her voice turned cold. "The same thing that is going to happen to *my mom*," she said, "if she comes into the forest looking for me. I am not sitting up here safe waiting for my mom to turn into a decoy for that *thing*. So, yes, I'll take my chances. Besides," she added, "now *you* can distract the snake."

"Bud, she's not wrong," said Brian reluctantly. He knew better than Phil how quick Coco could be, and how brave. "Be careful, Tiny," he told her.

Tiny was the nickname he first gave her months ago. She'd hated it then, because she hated being small. But now Coco knew she wasn't small, not in the ways that counted, and Brian knew she knew. She rolled her eyes and flashed Brian a shaky grin.

Phil looked from Brian to Coco, opened his mouth, closed it again, and finally just nodded. "Be careful," he said to Coco.

"Yup," she said. "Be distracting."

It took a lot of flaming pine cones and shouting to keep the snake from noticing Coco as she crept down the other side of the tree. Brian just hoped Coco's mom couldn't hear the racket, all the way on the beach. The snake was so big the pine cones mostly just bounced off without disturbing it. An ordinary snake would have just crawled away.

But finally the snake locked onto them, staring. And when the twentieth or so flaming pine cone bounced off its head, it *hissed*. Phil had fantastic aim.

Coco dropped from branch to branch. Brian dropped lower too, if not quite so low.

"Hey!" he shouted at the snake. "Hey, you! Fangy! Look up here! Here!"

Its eyes were fixed on him, narrow and calculating. Brian wondered, staring into those weird eyes, if Phil was right and he had caught the thing's baby, fishing.

If this was personal. But that would be weird. Snakes hatched from eggs, and they didn't *parent*. Then again, snakes didn't sink sailboats either.

Coco was creeping towards the bundle of logs. At the same moment, the snake lunged up the tree. Brian discovered, fortunately, that his branch was just out of range.

Phil threw more pine cones. It was going well. It was going well right up until Coco had the bundle of wood slung across her shoulders, looking small under its weight. She began to creep back to the tree.

And a stick cracked, loudly, under her shoe.

The snake's head whipped around, mouth open, teeth glistening with black venom. It darted at her head, and Coco dodged, looking tiny and terrified.

And Phil yelled, something pretty close to a scream, grabbed the last flaming pine cone, and pitched it down with a lot of force and accuracy right onto the thing's eye. The monster left Coco and lunged upward for them, coming up just short.

By then, Coco had darted into the tree and was hustling upward. Brian and Phil were bellowing the worst things they could think of at the snake.

Coco rejoined them. She was pale and panting, and she had the bundle of logs on her back. "Phil, you saved my life," she said.

Phil looked startled. "I did? I guess I did," he said, looking both puzzled and pleased with himself. "Gotta make last year up to you somehow."

She smiled at him. "I think you did."

Brian was already busy jabbing as many fishhooks into the dry wood as he could, trying to make a proper missile.

"Okay," he said, "here," and handed Phil the first log, spiky with fishhooks.

Phil hefted it like it was the first pitch of the playoffs. He took a deep breath and threw. It shot straight down and smashed the snake right in the face. The snake recoiled, its massive mouth open, hissing.

"That's for my uncle!" bellowed Phil triumphantly.

The next piece of wood Brian lit on fire. The wood was paper-dry, and it only took a few moments to have a streamer of flame going steadily at one end, burning his fingers when he handed it over. Phil threw it down. "That's for the *Cassie!*" he roared. Coco was on her feet, cheering, clinging to an overhead branch two-handed.

Now the snake was really enraged, and instead of leaving, as any sensible animal would do, it lunged higher yet, wrapping its body around the trunk of the tree, jaws going wide. Brian had to pull the sleeve of his wool sweater over his hand to grip the next log, to keep his skin from burning.

Phil pitched the log straight into the snake's open mouth. Brian saw the flame, glimmering as it fell, illuminating all the rows of teeth and the cotton-pink throat. Then the jaws slammed shut and the snake recoiled, all the way back down to the ground.

They waited, gasping, for it to come up after them again. But the snake had had enough. It retreated, uncoiling from the tree and disappearing into the dark.

They looked at each other.

"Is it gone?" said Phil. "Did we win?"

"I don't see it," said Coco, peering. "Phil, that was awesome."

Phil glowed.

Brian hesitated, following the silver line of the serpent as it vanished into the island's whispering murk. "We won," he said slowly. "But I'm pretty sure we won't win the big prize until we get off this island. Let's get back to the beach."

13

THEY RAN FOR the beach as fast as they could, straining their eyes and ears, picking up the remainder of the firewood as they went, keeping close together. The axe that Brian had carried away from the cabin was gone, although the firewood was where he dropped it. What did that mean? Had the axe man picked it up? But where was he now? Where had the snake gone? Brian didn't know. They didn't see or hear anything of the snake or the axe man all the way down to the beach.

It was almost full dark when they burst out of the woods. The light had gone purple, and rain spattered down. Phil ran in front, and Brian brought up the rear. Coco was in between.

Brian, despite everything, was happy to have Phil with them. As though, with Phil on the team, a piece of his life had finally joined another piece.

Ollie and Ms. Zintner were sitting by the fire. They had built it up so that it roared and crackled in the darkness, lit up a swath of the shore, and threw orange light on their faces. Brian was glad to see it. The fire seemed like an ally against the night and the island's known and unknown dangers. Phil, Brian, and Coco burst out of the woods and came clattering down onto the beach in a shower of small, rolling rocks.

"There you are!" cried Ms. Zintner.

"Mom!" said Coco. She ran over and hugged her mother tightly.

"Where were you?" demanded Ms. Zintner, hugging Coco back. "This isn't a game, sweetie! I was worried sick. I nearly went into the woods after you. But—" She paused.

Brian already knew why she hadn't gone anywhere. He had caught sight of Ollie and her dad. Ollie had barely looked up when they came pelting across the beach. Ollie's mouth was in a thin line, and her dad was hallucinating.

He was still sitting upright against the rock. His arm was black and swollen nearly to the elbow. And he was talking, but nothing he said made any sense.

"Remember the goblin," he muttered. "To the west. The *west*. There were twelve when they came ashore." His eyes saw beyond her. "Six in the water now." His breathing was noisy. "Five got away. One still here. They're waiting for him. Listen to the chimes."

"He's been like this for an hour," said Ollie, with a shake in her voice. "But nothing makes sense."

One thing does, thought Brian. *The chimes.*

Phil put some of their dry wood carefully onto the fire. Flames shot up even higher. The bubble of warmth spread out to wrap them all. Coco put her hands out to the flames with a sigh.

"Any sign of a boat?" Phil said.

"No," said Ms. Zintner. She glanced at the untroubled lake. Brian followed her gaze. The Adirondacks were just blacker smudges against a charcoal sky. He couldn't see any lights onshore.

"The radio isn't working," Ms. Zintner went on. She didn't sound annoyed at Coco anymore. She just sounded worried. "And I don't understand why we haven't seen a boat. This isn't some tiny atoll in the middle of the ocean! It's a good-sized island in the middle of a busy lake!"

Brian wasn't surprised. Coco's mouth just pressed down in a grim line. Brian thought again, with a feeling like a cold finger scraping down his spine, of the axe man's laughter. *No one's coming,* he thought. *We're behind the mist, we're in the land of the lake monster. Mr. Dimmonds couldn't find this island on his map. We're on our own. We have to get ourselves off somehow. But we don't have a boat. We don't have any food. What do we do?*

He had no idea. Coco said, "Mom, the monster—the thing that sank the *Cassie*—we found a snakeskin. We—it comes on land."

Ms. Zintner looked doubtful.

"I got a piece of it," said Phil unexpectedly, and he pulled out a strip of the shed skin, passing it to Ms. Zintner. Brian hadn't even seen him pick it up.

Coco's mom stared from the evidence to her daughter. "Oh, my word," she said. "This—doesn't make any sense. Water snakes—or whatever—they don't . . ."

"This one does," said Coco. Both boys nodded confirmation. "But we've got a lot of firewood now," Coco added. "We think—we hope—it won't come near a fire. But it's big—really big. We have to keep watch. And there's a man—"

Coco told a highly edited version of their adventures. Brian could tell she was struggling between honesty and not distressing her mom.

But maybe she said too much. "There's someone else on this island?" demanded Coco's mom. "Well, that's great news! He has a boat certainly. And probably a radio . . ." She was already reaching again for their silent radio.

"No, Mom," said Coco reluctantly. "I don't—I don't think he's in his right mind. He's got an axe. He was—he said some bad things to us. I don't think he wants to help."

Coco's mom frowned. "So you're saying that there is a giant, boat-sinking snake on this island, and also a disturbed man with an axe."

"Um, yeah," said Coco, her voice small.

"Whew," said her mother. "Well, the snake can't be too dangerous if the man with the axe is still around."

Brian and Coco exchanged glances. "I think we should still keep an eye out tonight," said Brian firmly. "And keep the fire going."

"I'm with you there, Brian," said Ms. Zintner. "I'm glad you're okay."

At that moment, a faint rumble of thunder sounded against the far horizon, and the very light drizzle thickened. *It absolutely can't rain,* Brian thought, sinking down onto a rock beside Ollie and pulling the hood of his jacket over his head. *That would be the final straw.* He wasn't sure if he was more uncomfortable putting his back to the forest or to the water.

"Stay close to the fire tonight, everyone," said Ms. Zintner. "Look out for a boat. And tomorrow—we can decide what to do."

Ms. Zintner handed around squares of chocolate and granola bars from the emergency kit. While they were in the woods, she'd also filled a bottle of water and purified it with the iodine tablets. It was chemical-tasting but better than nothing. Between them they drained it dry, and then Ms. Zintner went down to the lake to refill it.

Brian thought he saw a strange ripple in the water. It might have been a trick of rain and faint light, but . . . "Wait!" he said. Coco's mom was right at their edge of the ring of firelight.

She paused. "What is it, Brian?"

Brian wasn't sure what he'd seen. And they *did* need more water. But he said, "I'm not sure that's a good idea."

Coco's mom said, "Brian, we need to hydrate." She shined her flashlight on the water. "I don't see anything."

"Me either," Brian admitted. "But . . ."

He scooped up a fist-sized rock from where he was sitting near the water and tossed it in.

Nothing.

"At least take a torch down with you," said Coco suddenly. She got up, lit a piece of wood, and went down to the water beside her mom, holding the fire in front of her. Stillness, silence. Nothing. But Brian still had the creepy feeling of being watched, as though there were eyes under the water, just out of range of the light.

Coco's mom bent to fill the bottle.

At that moment, Mr. Adler's eyes shot wide, but he wasn't looking at them. He was hallucinating again. "Twelve men survived the goblin," he said. "But they wished they hadn't. The island kept them. Until it didn't." He was silent for a few minutes, his uninjured fingers twitching. Then he cried, "He's got an axe!" and fell silent again.

They had all turned toward Mr. Adler. Except for Phil, who, wisely, had kept his eyes on the water. "Hey!" he screamed suddenly. *"Hey! Look!"*

Coco spun around, still holding her torch, just in time to illuminate filmy eyes just under the water and a mouth slowly opening . . . Coco's mom gasped and jumped back, pulling Coco with her, and the frilled, dripping head vanished almost as soon as it appeared. They scrambled over to the fire, looking shaken. The water bottle was maybe a quarter full.

It's waiting, Brian thought. *Hunting. We have to get out of here.*

"Okay," said Ms. Zintner, jaw set determinedly. She still had her arm around Coco. "No going near the lake, guys; this water has got to last. Maybe we can collect some rain in the lifeboat. Here, Phil, Brian, help me spread it out."

They tried to arrange the deflated lifeboat so that it would capture a bit of rain. Brian was wrestling with the heavy rubber when Ollie spoke:

"Dad?" said Ollie, with a crack in her voice. Her dad had fallen silent, his eyes half-open, fixed on the lake. He turned his head and looked at her when she spoke, but his eyes hardly seemed to see her. Coco went and put both arms around Ollie. Brian went to sit on Coco's other side, as near the two girls as he could get.

And then Phil, surprising Brian, got up and went and sat down near them all as well. "Ollie, I'm really sorry," he said.

"Thanks, guys," said Ollie, in a small voice. She didn't, Brian noticed, look at her watch. Which was weird in itself. When Ollie was in trouble, she *always* looked at her watch. She looked from her dad to the lake, brows drawn together.

They sat still for a few moments, watching the lake, watching the fire. No one said anything. Phil started experimenting with roasting a granola bar. The air around their campfire started to smell vaguely like toast.

Coco said, "Oh, look—I forgot about this." She reached into her jacket pocket and pulled out the black book from the cabin. She turned it gently, over and over, in her hands. It was a weather-stained, leather-bound old book, cracked around the edges.

"But what is it?" asked Phil.

Coco passed the book to Brian. Brian loved books. He touched the cover reverently and then opened it. The others peered over his shoulder. "I think—it looks like a ship's log," he said.

Capt. Wm. Sheehan, said the log, *of the* Goblin *out of Burlington. Thomas Ross, first mate.*

Sheehan, thought Brian. *That rings a bell. And* Goblin. *Mr. Adler said something about a goblin . . .*

Frowning, he tried to remember where he'd heard the name Sheehan.

Oh. *Hauntings and Horrors in the Green Mountain State.* Sheehan had been a smuggler, right? And a ship called the *Goblin.* But they'd foundered. Lost with all hands. Hadn't they?

There was a faint crack of thunder. Lines of cold foam marked the lake. It was cold, even with the fire and the emergency blankets. Even pressed close together, they were all shivering.

Brian picked up the flashlight and turned it onto the pages of the log. He squinted. The writing was spidery and faded. The first entries were, apparently, about the weather and the cargo the ship was carrying. Then . . .

Thursday, 10 November 1808

Hole found below the waterline at eight bells.
Cause unknown. Mr. Jim Bartlett, sailor, lost
overboard in the night. Winds out of the north,
cold after sunset, moderate squall, wind to the
SSE. Cargo half full, setting course to return to
port for repairs.

Friday, 11 November 1808

Sighted an unknown island off the larboard bow
in thick fog. Did not know there was an uncharted
island of such size anywhere in this part of the
lake. The men are unsettled, say the island is
cursed. Many unhappy over the death of Bartlett,
who was much liked. But I've given orders to close
with the land. At good anchor, in shallow water,
we might come at the leak without returning to
port. We shan't get very many more hauls before
the lake freezes.
Anchored. Heaved down the ship to come at the
leak, only to find that it had gained against all
expectations, that the hold was awash.
Mr. Will Scott, sailor, lost in the hold under
mysterious circumstances. We pumped at the water

151

and heaved down the Goblin to come at the leak.
Named the land Deadman's Island, for Bartlett
and Scott, added it to our charts.

Monday, 14 November 1808

Patched the leak and made sail for Otter Creek to
pick up cargo. Revenue cutter was warned. We
fled, and cutter Fly pursued.
Shaped return course for Deadman's Isle, with the
wind fair, thinking to lose cutter in the awkward
shoals and hide the ship inshore. Thick fog on the
water.
Came up in the shallows in full dark, run aground
(as we thought) with the ship leaking. Immediately
the Goblin began to settle. With no chance of
saving her, gave the orders to abandon ship; we put
out the lifeboats and made for shore.

Here, the precise, spidery writing grew hasty and
scribbled, and there were spatters of ink on the page, as
though the writer had lost control of the pen, in their
hurry to write.

Were nearly on the beach when monstrous sight
met my eyes.

Brian and Coco glanced at each other. Phil, reading over their shoulders, shivered.

A vast head, like the head of an asp. A beast like a snake, like a fish, like both, and like neither. The fog had cleared, and the beast was mirror-silver in the moonlight, with water dripping from its jaws. It plunged, tore the Goblin *to pieces, like a terrier with a rat, writhing so that the water was beaten to white foam.*
Pulled the boat up above the high-water mark. Stared and stared at the water until the shining silver line of the monster was quite gone and all that was left was scattered wreckage from the poor, stricken Goblin. *Of the crew only twelve of us came ashore.*

There was a page that simply contained a drawing of the lake monster plunging down into the hold of the *Goblin*. It was faded and water-stained but still unmistakable.

Brian stopped reading.

"Oh my God," said Coco's mother reverently.

"Keep going," said Phil.

The next few entries were ruined by stains. It picked up, Brian noted, nearly a week later.

Sunday, 20 November 1808

*Why do they not see us? We thought, of course,
that our stay on the island would be brief. We
should be in easy view of any number of fishing
vessels. Indeed, we have seen a few at a distance,
by day. But though we have cut trees and burned
them like madmen from the beach in our fury, it
avails us nothing. Tommy has been marvelous,
encouraging the crew. But it cannot last.*

Tuesday, 22 November 1808

*The slow horror of this island is creeping up on us all,
and I have trouble keeping up the spirits of the men.
All around lie signs of rude, makeshift habitations.
We have made one ourselves: a rough cabin, to house
us out of the wet. There are bones in the forest, a grave
or two, carvings on trees. We cannot help but feel that
we are not the first to live here. Live here? How is that
possible? Even without boats, one may merely walk
across the lake four months out of the year.
And yet.
And yet.
We are afraid.*

Saturday, 3 December 1808

> *Full moon tonight, the nineteenth day of our*
> *marooning. Marooned in Lake Champlain, has*
> *that ever happened before? Of course, we've*
> *the boats, but the men are afraid to brave the*
> *monster's waters in an open boat, when the*
> *Goblin herself could not prevail.*

Sunday, 4 December 1808

> *Yesterday, Michael Flanagan, sailor, lost while*
> *attempting to cast a fishing line just offshore.*
> *The monstrous snake reared up out of the water*
> *and snatched him. Only six of us left. I have*
> *forbidden fishing, for the time being, but it cannot*
> *last, for we are hungry . . .*

"Oh my God," said Coco's mom again. "A record—documentary proof—of a lake monster in Lake Champlain. Champ. It existed."

"Exists," Coco corrected her mother. She, with greater experience of strange occurrences, seemed preoccupied by a different aspect of the story of Captain Wm. Sheehan and the crew of the *Goblin*.

Brian was too. His eyes met hers.

"He says they couldn't get off," she said low, just to Brian, in a tone of someone confirming what she'd already suspected.

Brian just nodded.

"We have to get off somehow. Can we build a boat?" Coco asked him.

"No," he said. "Not even a raft. We don't have any tools. We'd have to . . ." His voice failed him. He rallied and went on. "Um, wait until the lake freezes. If it freezes; it doesn't freeze every year anymore. Climate change. And if it did freeze, it would be in January at the earliest. Months from now."

"But do you think it's the same snake?" asked Phil, pointing at the log. "The same one that sank the *Goblin*?" His freckled face was smudged and pale. "A two-hundred-year-old snake?"

"Surely not," said Coco's mom.

Brian wasn't so sure himself.

"It might reproduce," said Coco. "You did catch a little snake. Maybe it has eggs."

"There would need to be two of them, then," said Phil, looking fascinated.

Brian thought that one giant snake was plenty. He turned a page in the log.

Wednesday, 4 January 1809

Mutiny. Half the men wish to launch the lifeboats
afresh. Half go in mortal fear of the serpent. I
have counseled patience, since it will not be too
many weeks—or even days—before the lake has
frozen solid. But it is true we are cold and hungry
here, all the more maddening, since Burlington is a
half day distant, under easy sail.
Unable to control the men, I have allowed the
launch of a boat. No provisions, since if they
succeed, they will not need them.
And if they fail, we desperately will.

Thursday, 5 January 1809

Grieved to report the destruction of the lifeboat
Emily, with all hands. They were under moderate
sail, course ESE, when we watchers onshore saw
a wave come up, and then a glitter, and then a
smashing sound as the boat was flung into the air.
The men came down into the water, and they had no
chance even to drown, for the serpent plucked them
out like so many fish and swallowed them down.
Appended is a list of the lost men.

Three of us remain: myself, William Sheehan,
captain; Thomas Ross, first mate; and James Allen,
seaman. We are resolved to stay on this island
until the lake has frozen solidly and then, when
there is no fear of the serpent breaking through the
ice, we will walk back to Burlington. We cut wood
like madmen by day and tend the fire by night
that keeps the serpent from our door. But we are
mortally hungry.

Friday, 6 January 1809

Have settled the single remaining lifeboat into cave
near the landing site, marked location on chart.
Rations are low, and it is very cold. Morale poor
among the three of us, although Tommy does what
he can, with jokes and songs, God bless that man.
The water has not frozen yet; it has been a winter
of rain thus far, without snow. Sometimes, Tommy
says, the lake has frozen solid as late as March. Pray.

Sunday, 8 January 1809

We are hunted now. We hear the sound of the
creature in the night; the cabin is besieged.

We thought it would go quiet with the frost, like any animal. We thought it would retreat beneath the lake and leave us be. But it has not. We see its track in the mud. We have hung all metal we possess, all the fishhooks that do us no good, to give us a little warning by chiming together, for the creature often hunts from above. We cut wood all day and burn it all night. We see its eyes shine just outside the firelight.

Even Tommy cannot joke anymore.

We cannot use the boat, and the lake hasn't frozen yet. It ought to be frozen long since, but it isn't.

As though some malign force keeps it liquid.

As though the ordinary rules of creation are suspended and we live at the serpent's whim, like mice in a giant larder. We cannot get out. We will have to kill it, we think. We've no weapons but a couple of knives and my axe. Tommy and Jim are afraid. But what choice do we have?

We hear the scales sliding at night now, every night, as the creature comes closer. Closer, closer. We do not often see it. But we know it is there. Waiting. We are hungry, and weak. We must make our last stand soon, while our strength holds. Pray.

The last sentence ended with a splatter and a scrawl. As though the writer had run out of ink and then been distracted by something else and not gone back.

They all looked at each other. "I wonder what happened to them?" said Coco softly.

Eaten, Brian thought. Coco's mom had slipped away to the radio, *again.*

Brian added, low, "I wonder who the axe man is? And the—the person on the bed?"

"Maybe the skeleton was Sheehan," said Coco. "That would make sense. He wrote the log and the skeleton was holding it." She shivered at the thought.

Phil said, with dawning horror, "But—if Sheehan and the crew got stuck here, and the axe man got stuck here too . . . are we stuck here?"

Brian took a breath. *Yeah,* he was going to say. *Yeah, we are. Until we figure out how to . . .* But he was stopped by Ollie's dad, speaking sharply. "Olivia!" he cried, once, in a such a tone of lucid terror that they all whipped around, and Coco's mom got up and hurried back toward them. Then Mr. Adler's voice dropped, feeble, still afraid. "Don't—don't."

"Wait," said Phil. "Where's Ollie?"

All of them turned to look, scattering pebbles.

Ollie wasn't anywhere. Ollie was gone.

"When did she go?" asked Brian.

"She said something about going to pee," said Coco. "I thought she was going just a few steps, like the rest of us did."

Brian shined the emergency flashlight. It lit up starkly the white, sweating face of Mr. Adler, his eyes stretched wide open, and two tears running down his temples to mix with the sweat. His lips were cracking.

No Ollie.

"Ollie!" yelled Coco. "Ollie!"

Why—what could possibly make her go off by herself, with a giant snake loose and her dad here, sick? What—

Or had something grabbed her? Brian wondered, cold to his bones. No—they'd have noticed. Wouldn't they?

"Ollie!" they all shouted.

Silence. Only a faint wind, high up, whispered through the pines, and rocks groaned with the slight movement of the lake, back and forth. It was very cold now, and the stars were coming out.

"No," Ollie's dad muttered. His voice was fading. His breathing sounded horrible. "No, I won't. Never. Never never—"

Then someone kicked a rock behind them; Brian spun, along with the others. His heart beat high and fast in his throat.

Rocks rolled down the steep slope of the beach. They all stiffened, looking for the silver gleam of the beast in the shadows—and then Ollie's voice, reassuring, was calling back, "It's me. I'm fine."

Not just reassuring; she sounded steadier than she'd sounded since the *Cassandra* sank. She was running back toward them, her feet quick on the rolling rocks.

"Ollie," whispered her dad, and *he* didn't sound steady at all; his voice was full of a strange, vague horror.

"Ollie," said Coco, in a voice that didn't even sound like herself, it was so frightened and angry. "Where were you?"

Ollie didn't say anything, just knelt at once down beside her dad. "Hey," she said to him. And to Coco, without turning her head, she said, "I had to pee. Calm down."

Ms. Zintner said, "Ollie, you know better than to wander off without telling anyone."

"Yep," said Ollie. "I do." She didn't sound sorry at all. "How's it going, Dad?" She glanced from his face to her watch.

Coco said suddenly, "Ollie, that countdown. How long do we still have?"

"Oh?" said Ollie. "Oh, that. That's okay. It's stopped now."

She busied herself over her dad and didn't say anything else about it. Brian thought, *There's something she's not telling us.*

"What did you do?" Ollie's dad was whispering. "Ollie. I saw him. What did you do?"

"I had to pee, Dad," said Ollie. "You didn't see anything. You're very sick."

Was she lying? Brian wasn't sure. Ollie was a good liar. And he couldn't see her face. Just her silhouette against the starlit water as she handed her dad the water bottle. But why would she lie to them? She wouldn't. Also, where would she have gone? There wasn't anywhere *to* go.

"No," said Ollie's dad, turning his head away. "Ollie, no. I *saw* him. I saw him, and he said—"

"Dad," said Ollie, gently and firmly. She sounded like the grown-up, calm and a little sad, and for some reason, that scared Brian. "You're just hallucinating. Drink some water. Water is super important. That's what you always tell me, right? Gotta hydrate . . ."

He was staring up at her face and seemed almost lucid. "I was—I was dreaming?" he said. "I—but he—seemed real."

"There's no one here but us," said Ollie.

"Okay," said her dad. Ollie helped him drink out of the water bottle.

He drank and drank and gasped. "That's *vile*. What's up with the water?" His voice sounded stronger than it had all evening. Brian felt a surge of hope. Maybe Mr. Adler would be okay!

163

"Iodine," said Ollie. Her eyes never left her dad's face. "There was emergency iodine in the survival pack on the lifeboat. Gotta be safe, and drink clean water. Dad—you sound better. Are you better?"

Mr. Adler wiped his mouth. He looked up. "Where are we?" he said. He *did* sound better. "I—I've been having such weird dreams. Where's the *Cassandra*?"

"Roger, you sound so much better!" said Coco's mom. "We've been worried."

He gave her a rather tired smile. "I feel better," said Mr. Adler. Ollie was sitting back on her heels, watching.

"Mr. Adler?" Coco said. "Are you okay?"

"I think so," he said, sitting up. "But it's all kind of a blur. Fill me in, guys."

"Well," said Ollie. "We're stuck on an island in the middle of Lake Champlain with a giant snake and a man with an axe, and we have to figure out how to get off."

14

TAKING TURNS, PHIL, Coco, and Brian filled Mr. Adler in. About the axe man, about the snake, about the cabin and the ship's log. Brian and Coco didn't try to explain about ghosts, but they told everything else. Ollie's dad listened quietly, with Ollie tucked against his side like a little kid. When they weren't talking, Brian and Coco and Phil took turns putting wood onto the fire. Their woodpile, Brian thought nervously, would *probably* last until dawn, but it was going to be close.

And after that, he had no idea what to do.

Brian kept covertly staring at Mr. Adler, all the while they were talking. He couldn't figure it out. Half an hour ago, Ollie's dad had looked like he was about to *die*. Not that Brian wasn't overjoyed. He was. The thought of Ollie losing her dad—of all of them losing Mr. Adler—had been almost unbearable.

But the weirdest thing was that Ollie didn't seem surprised. Or even that happy. No—of course she was happy. She didn't let go of her dad for a second. But not *delighted*, not—something. She wasn't reacting the way he would have expected her to.

Something, Brian thought, was wrong.

And he wasn't the only one to think that. He could tell by Coco's narrow-eyed expression that she was puzzled too. But they couldn't exactly bring it up in front of everyone. How would he even ask? *Ollie, why aren't you happier?* So he didn't say anything.

They finished their story, and Mr. Adler was silent for a moment. In the silence, Brian heard a log crumbling into itself on the fire, and he reached to put on more wood. Then Mr. Adler said, "I remember getting bit." He looked down at his hand. "But everything else is a blur. I'm sorry about Dane."

Phil said, "Uncle Dane found his lake monster. He wanted that more than anything."

They were all quiet then.

"And a man on the island?" said Mr. Adler. "He threatened you with an axe? How dare he?" He held Ollie tighter. "Well, at least we're not alone, although a disturbed, armed man is not really what you'd hope for. I think we'd better sit tight until morning in any case.

You all can go to sleep, I can keep watch for a bit. Feel fit as a fiddle. Must have metabolized the snake venom."

"What I don't understand," Ms. Zintner broke in, "is that I've been signaling *all afternoon*. We fired off an emergency smoke signal! And now we've got this campfire—but no one, not a soul on the lake, has shown up. *And* the radio doesn't work." She glared at it.

But right as she said that, the radio crackled to life.

It frizzed with static. Then there was the unmistakable sound of someone breathing. Ms. Zintner jumped for the handpiece. "Mayday, Mayday, do you read? We are the survivors of the wreck of the *Cassandra* requesting immediate assistance . . ."

She waited. They all waited. But the voice on the radio didn't say anything. It was just breathing. Over the sound of heaving, staticky breaths, Brian heard the ripple of the water, the grind of rocks being turned over and over in the endless churn of the lake.

The radio began crackling. *"Captain,"* said the radio. *"Give me the captain."* This time, Ms. Zintner just stared at it.

"Give me the captain," said the radio, and it sighed, soft and sad. *"He's waited so long. Give me the captain. Or die. Die like us.*

"Die die die diediedieieie."

The radio cut out again, with a shower of static.

Coco bit down hard on her lower lip.

Mr. Adler said, after a pause, "There is obviously someone mentally ill playing with the radio frequency. Maybe the man with the axe. Does it sound like him?"

"No," said Coco. "No, it doesn't." No one else said anything.

Mentally ill maybe, thought Brian. *But no one is playing.*

"We can't do anything tonight," Ms. Zintner said firmly, after the radio had been silent for half an hour. The small spattering rain had started up again, and no one was particularly comfortable. The moon hung low over the mountains, making a trail of silver on the lake. "You should sleep. Especially you, Roger. You have been very sick."

Brian had pulled the bandage away from Mr. Adler's arm to check the punctures. To his surprise, the black swelling had faded from his arm; the holes themselves were scabbing over. The skin was a little red and puffy right around the holes, but not bad, not worse than a spider bite. It was as though they'd imagined the black swelling, the leaking fluid, Mr. Adler's eyes gone glassy . . .

He rebandaged the punctures, wondering if he should say anything. Ollie sure didn't. She was still leaning on her dad, quiet, staring out at the water.

He and Phil and Coco finally wound up huddled on the other side of the fire, wrapped tightly in one emergency blanket. It was neither dry nor warm nor comfortable, but it was a little better than just the bare rocks. They whispered to each other.

"I think the grown-ups are going to want to stay close to shore and keep trying to signal tomorrow," said Coco. "But I don't think it will do any good."

"No," said Brian, whispering back. "Whatever happened to Sheehan—it happened to us too. No one's coming for us. It's the world behind the mist all over again. The world behind the mirror."

"Behind what mirror?" said Phil.

"Long story," said Brian.

"Fine. But if no one's coming," said Phil, with a shake in his voice, "what do we do? We don't have a boat! And we don't have food! Or any way to get food! If we can't get off—then we'll die!"

His voice went a little shrill.

Coco said suddenly, "They had a boat." Coco was between them, huddled down in the emergency blanket. They could hardly see more of her than the top of her damp, pinkish head.

Brian stared at her, not sure he'd heard correctly. Phil had stopped talking in surprise.

"Sheehan and his men, I mean," Coco said, muffled. She poked her head up. "The one they hid. In the cave. Somewhere. Remember? He mentioned it in the log."

"But," said Brian, objecting, "they hid it over two hundred years ago! Wouldn't it have rotted?"

This time Phil answered, eyes narrowing. "Not if it was a good boat to begin with. Especially if they put it in a cave. Temperature-stable, you know. Even if it got wet sometimes, that would only swell the timbers and make it watertight."

Brian felt a sneaking flare of hope.

"But," said Coco, "even if there is a boat—how do we find it? The log didn't say where, exactly. Just a cave, near the shore. We could walk around this island for weeks before we found it. I mean—the cave might be overgrown, or whatever." She hesitated. And then she added, "I don't think we have weeks."

"No," said Brian. "I don't even think we have days."

Neither of the others objected. They were silent awhile, thinking.

Then Phil said, "I wonder what the axe man knows?" Then he answered himself. "Probably nothing. If he knew there was a boat, why would he still be here?"

Brian and Coco looked at each other. *He's here because he's a ghost,* they were both thinking.

"We should talk to him," said Brian.

15

THE NEXT DAY dawned frigid and damply cold, with a high wind blowing and the sun of the day before a distant memory. The pale buds tossed back and forth on the black-branched trees, and Brian would have given almost anything to stay on the beach and wait for a boat, rather than go back into the forest. The forest with its mud, its monster, and its axe-wielding stranger. Its fishhooks and its cabin and the feeling of long, cold despair. It felt like a trap. At least on the beach you could see the horizon, you could *hope* for a boat, for a rescue that was quick and easy and painless.

But Brian had seen enough of strange spaces, of small, haunted worlds, to know by now that there were no miracles, no easy escapes. That they'd have to smash their own way out.

They had chocolate and lake water and a few handfuls of spruce tips for breakfast. They'd collected a little rain in the night, but their water bottle was only half full. Mr. Adler threw a few spruce tips into the water, to hide the taste of purifying iodine. Brian eyed the bottle with misgiving. There were five of them, after all. But what were they going to do? None of them felt safe going back to the lake for refills.

At least Mr. Adler was better. He woke up looking cheerful; he ate his granola bar as happily as he'd gobbled pancakes and bacon back in Evansburg. The sight almost made Brian smile. Mr. Adler was a morning person even when he'd nearly died of a lake monster bite.

Coco's mom was looking tired; Brian didn't think she'd slept. She'd been watching the lake and the fire and the woods, keeping an eye out for the lake monster and the axe man.

Brian reopened Sheehan's log, squinting to see its pages in the flat morning light. Coco looked over his shoulder. Phil was peeing behind a rock. Ollie sat still, watching the lake. Brian wondered why Ollie wasn't more curious, and he was struck again by the thought, *There's something she's not telling us.*

Coco said, "It just says a cove, where they hid the boat. But which cove? Where?"

"He may have made a chart," said Brian. "And hid it somewhere. Separate from the log. Or maybe a page of the log got torn out. Dunno. We'll have to go back to the cabin. It's at least a place to start looking." He took a breath. "And I'd rather talk to the axe man than the monster. I don't see a lot of other options."

Coco said, after a pause, "Neither do I. Unfortunately."

They gathered around their dying fire. Phil had already thrown on the final log; their wood had lasted the night, just, but they didn't have any for another night. They were all exhausted, pinched-pale with cold. Coco's teeth were chattering continually now, even though they'd all slept piled like puppies, uncomfortably, so near the fire that smoke stung their eyes and noses, and wrapped as best they could be in one emergency blanket. All three of their faces were smudged with soot.

Ollie's dad said ruefully, "Water and granola bars for breakfast, Ollie-pop. I wish it were pancakes."

"Piney iodine water," said Ollie, and smiled at him. "I don't mind."

Ollie, Brian thought. *You look sad. Happy and sad. Why?*

The silence from the forest was thick and heavy. But not, Brian thought, empty. He wondered what was going to happen.

"Ollie," said her dad softly. "You're as brave as your mother."

Ollie's smile was the first real one Brian had seen from his friend in a while. "No way," she said. "No one's as brave as Mom."

"Nope, no one else in the world," said her dad, weirdly serious. "Except you."

Ollie smiled. But she also glanced down at her watch, turning her hand just enough that Brian could read the word, there and gone on the watch face.

DONT, the watch said.

Ollie, what are you up to?

———

The kids had to convince the adults that *no, really, we don't think a boat is coming.* Ms. Zintner took some convincing.

"Mom," said Coco, while Mr. Adler, the good camper, carefully smothered the last of the fire with rocks and dirt. "Sheehan and the people from the *Goblin* couldn't get a boat to pick them up. And they were here for *months.*"

"But that was over two hundred years ago," her mom pointed out, not unreasonably. "The lake has changed a bit since then, you know."

"Yeah," said Coco. "But no one saw the smoke signal yesterday or our fire last night. Just like no one saw the signals from the survivors of the *Goblin*. Maybe—there might be—an atmospheric condition that makes this island hard to see. If there's a boat on this island, it's better to go look for it than just *wait*. We don't have enough firewood for tonight, anyway. Or food." She sounded certain, and fierce.

Ms. Zintner eyed her daughter as though seeing her for the first time. "Coco," she said, sounding a little puzzled. "You've grown up a lot this year."

Coco looked surprised.

"All of you have," put in Ollie's dad, looking up from the remains of their campfire. "We were so worried about how all of you had changed that we didn't stop to celebrate you growing up. Zelda, I think we should trust them. Kids, what do you think we should do?"

It had never occurred to Brian that all the terrifying things—the corn maze, the scarecrows, Mother Hemlock's malevolent face, and the smiling man—were anything but *bad*. Well, they were. But since all that had happened to him, he trusted himself more. He trusted his friends more. He could make a hard decision; he could do a dangerous thing. He could keep going even though he was afraid. That wasn't nothing.

He said, "I think we should try to find the boat."

The grown-ups looked at each other.

"Yeah," said Coco. "Let's find the boat."

They collected as much of their stuff as they could. The emergency kit, the first aid kit. They had a couple of granola bars left, but that was all. The empty water bottle was a bigger worry, though. Dehydration would get them much sooner than being hungry. Brian wondered if that was how the snake had gotten some of the crew of the *Goblin*. Once they'd made it harder for the snake to hunt from trees, it just lurked in the water like a crocodile. Waiting.

Phil said, "I don't remember how to get to the cabin. Do you?"

Brian said, "I think I do." He hoped he did. How big could the island be?

"Wonderful," said Mr. Adler calmly. "Brian, if you would lead the way, then?" He was carrying the first aid kit. Coco's mom carried the emergency kit. They'd talked about trying to roll up the punctured raft, but it was heavy and damp and not much good except as a makeshift tent. It certainly would never float again. You could patch a hole; you couldn't really patch a chunk missing.

The sun was pretty well up by the time they left. They hadn't wanted to creep around the forest right at dawn, in case the snake was hunting. But it didn't seem to actually brighten anything. The light was gray and flat; there was a haze on the lake. A little mist curled, visibly, between the trees of the forest. Brian didn't like it. But what choice did they have? Stay by the lake, hope the monster didn't nab them when they finally got desperate for water?

Brian took a deep breath and led them into the woods. Mr. Adler brought up the rear, with Ollie walking just ahead of him. Coco, her mom, and Phil were in between.

"Remember to look up," said Phil. The rest of them nodded.

They slipped between the pines and pushed uphill, back in the grip of the trees. The path climbed up and up, winding a little, as Brian worked hard to get his bearings. The air was cold in his nose and throat. All of them were scanning the woods. Waiting, thought Brian, for something to happen.

But it was not, in the end, the sound of the chimes or the movements of the snake that caught their attention. It was a voice.

It was the axe man's voice, and he wasn't singing this time. He was reciting a poem to himself. His words carried eerily through the trees, now shouting, now whispering, breaking the thick, birdless silence. They all stopped dead to listen, hardly breathing, trying to figure out where the voice was coming from.

Four times fifty living men,
(And I heard nor sigh nor groan)
With heavy thump, a lifeless lump,
They dropped down one by one.

The adults looked astonished.

"That's the axe man," whispered Coco to the grown-ups.

Unconsciously, they had all pressed closer together. The sound seemed like it was coming from everywhere and nowhere. The forest was cold and damp, but Brian was sweating under his clothes.

"I know that poem," said Coco's mom, listening, head tilted to one side. "I majored in English lit in college. That's 'The Rime of the Ancient Mariner.' A long, old poem. About a man who kills an albatross and brings bad luck on his crew."

"What happened to him?" Coco asked. "The man who kills the albatross?"

"Well, his crew died," said Ms. Zintner. "But—he didn't. He wanted to, you see. But he couldn't. Instead he was cursed to wander the world forever, telling his story."

Somewhere in the distance, the voice went stridently on, growing louder and louder.

Alone, alone, all, all alone
Alone on a wide wide sea—

The verse went on, but Ollie broke in softly, "I wonder what happened to Captain Sheehan?"

"The log doesn't say," said Brian. "It ended with them going to fight the snake."

Near and far away—it was hard to tell—the voice, which had faded a little, rose again, on part of a new verse:

Seven days, seven nights, I saw that curse,
And yet I could not die.

"Yeah," Coco said. "We need to find him."

"Cabin," said Brian. "We should still start with the cabin." Brian took a deep breath and scanned the woods again for landmarks. It was hard. The whispering voice and the flat, deceptive light distracted him. But he could do it, he told himself. He'd been hiking and camping in the woods since he was little.

Okay, he thought to himself. *Okay. The beach is back that way, the cabin must be . . .*

That way. He remembered that rise, the way the ground sloped, and . . . and there was the oak tree, and behind it . . .

"Hang on," said Coco's mom. "Did I hear a chime?"

They all paused to listen, every nerve strung tight. But there was only silence.

"Let's go on," said Ollie's dad at last. "Be careful, everyone."

They didn't so much enter the clearing with the cabin as it sort of *happened* to them; one moment they were in thick trees, going uncomfortably uphill, panting, sweating, and chilled all at once. The next moment, the trees opened up and the cabin was there, weathered gray, with its crooked door.

And from inside it came the axe man's whispering voice. The voice echoed and shrank, seemed to come now from the trees, now from the house.

"*I looked upon the rotting sea,*" he said. He sounded sad now, Brian thought.

> *And drew my eyes away;*
> *I looked upon the rotting deck,*
> *And there the dead men lay.*

Ollie stepped forward and knocked on the door.

The chanting voice cut off. Ollie called, her voice quiet but firm, "Are you Captain William Sheehan?"

Beside him, Brian felt the adults—who had been poised to step forward and say polite adult things—shut their mouths in surprise.

Silence from the cabin. Ollie had her hand raised to knock again.

Then, with no sound of footsteps, the door swung open. The axe man stood in the gap.

Brian felt, more than saw, the two adults recoil. It wasn't that the axe man looked horrible or anything. Yeah, his beard was long, his clothes were ragged. But it wasn't that. It was the look in his eyes. He looked old. And sad. And lost. He wasn't holding his axe. He was holding a skull between his hands.

"Here lies Tommy Ross," the axe man said, like an epitaph, looking down into the skull's empty eye sockets. "You should have left him alone. Why didn't you leave him alone? Why come here?"

"I'm sorry," said Brian. "Captain?"

"Yes," said the axe man. "Cap'n William Sheehan, master of the *Goblin*."

"Impossible," said Coco's mom. "He's got a mania—projecting."

"Wait, Mom," said Coco.

"It's you again," said Sheehan. He sounded sour. "Well, you disturbed Tommy, so I'm not going to axe you, after all. It would be too kind."

Brian said, "Sir, what happened to the men? The crew of the *Goblin*? We read the log. But it ends the night you went to fight the snake."

"I fought the snake," said Sheehan. His voice was dull, and his outline was—blurred somehow—to Brian. Like he was a rock that had been too long in water, all the edges worn away. "The others—I told them to go. To take the last boat. I thought—if I wounded the beast enough, it would stay in the water, it wouldn't get them. I thought maybe I could get Tommy out that way at least. Loved Tommy, don't you know. He was the best man I ever knew."

"Did Tommy go?" This was Phil, surprisingly, his voice steady, if a little bit uncertain.

Sheehan's voice turned angry. "I told the blasted fool to go. But he didn't. He said he'd never leave me. The snake got him." Sheehan glanced around the clearing. "He died in my arms. I put him in the cabin, so his bones would be safe, at least." His voice got angry again. "And they were, before you."

"What happened then?" Coco asked, gently.

Sheehan's eyes looked sunk in his head. "After Tommy died, I snatched up his axe, and I went out to bash the thing. Got in my licks, I did. But it bit me too and then took off. I chased it all the way down to the water. But it was too fast for me. It slid into the water. It wasn't dead. I tried to go back to Tommy . . ."

"But you died," said Ollie softly. "You died under the tree by the water, the one with the carving." Brian remembered the skull there. He supposed that Ollie was right.

"I guess I died," acknowledged the captain. A frown of concentration showed between his eyes. "It didn't seem to make much difference, though. I got up. Went to find the others. I hoped that the boys at least had taken the boat and gone."

His voice began to shake. "They hadn't. Not a one. They hadn't made it to the boat at all, they were just gone—swallowed whole, like rabbits.

"I went back to Tommy. Waited for the snake. Revenge, don't you know? I keep saying, now's the day, Bill old boy. But I'm afeared of her now. I'm so afraid, and Tommy made me brave last time, but Tommy won't talk to me anymore. But one day. One day. I'm waiting. I'm waiting!" He shouted the last word at the silent woods.

Suddenly he snatched up his axe, lying just inside the cabin door, still cradling Tommy's skull in his free hand. "No one should stay forever. No one, no one, and I'll axe you before I allow it. I will, I will . . ."

He raised his axe. Ms. Zintner shoved Coco behind her just as Mr. Adler said, "Kids, get back!"

But Brian's brain was racing. He saw the radio bobbing on Ms. Zintner's hip. He thought of the strange voice. *Give us the Captain,* he thought. It had sounded menacing. But maybe . . . maybe . . .

He reached forward, snatched the radio, and stepped around and in front of Mr. Adler before he could say anything. Brian's voice rose over everyone else's, strong and confident: "Captain, I think your men have been asking for you."

The captain stopped, as though he'd walked into a tree. The axe lowered. "What are you saying, boy?" he growled. "Tommy hasn't talked to me in oh so many days. Ever since I put him on that bed."

Brian didn't answer. Instead he held out the radio.

It immediately came to life, crackling in his hand. Captain Sheehan jerked back a step. "What's that?" he demanded, looking deeply suspicious. "What's that thing?"

Gathering his courage, Brian came forward, within range of the axe. The captain didn't swing it. The radio was still crackling.

"Listen," said Brian. "Listen."

Silence. For a moment, there was utter silence in that clearing, except for the sound of crackling. Brian's heart sank. He could be wrong. What if he was wrong?

But then a voice spoke from the radio:

"Bill," it said. *"Bill, is that you?"*

The captain stared. "Tom?" he said. *"Tom, where are you?"*

The hollow voice said, *"Waiting for you, in course. What's taking you so long?"*

"But, Tommy, I didn't kill the snake. I promised I would and I keep my promises."

"We're gone, Bill," said the soft voice on the radio. *"All of us are gone but you. It doesn't matter anymore. You did your best. You did enough for us. Enough for the old* Goblin. *Now, you just come along with me. You just come along."*

"I can't," whispered Bill. "Serpent's out there. I haven't killed it yet. That's what I meant to do. Kill it. But I was afraid."

"Not anymore," said the voice on the radio gently. *"Not anymore."*

Brian glanced sideways to see Ollie's face streaked and shining with tears. Her free hand had closed, white-knuckled, on her watch. There was so much jagged longing in the old captain's voice. And all of them understood what it was like to feel lonely, although maybe not as lonely as Captain Sheehan. And maybe all of them, but especially Brian, knew what it was like to feel as though you'd failed your friends.

But he hadn't. He knew that now. And maybe Sheehan was learning it too.

"Over the water, Bill. Into the moonlight," whispered the ghost on the radio. *"I was always close by, my dear. Always. Bill, it's time to rest now."*

The voice fell silent.

Complete silence in that clearing, in front of the lonely old cabin where a skeleton lay on the bed.

In that silence, they heard the ringing of metal. *The chimes,* Brian thought. *The fishhooks.*

"It's coming," whispered Phil.

They all spun around, with the cabin at their backs, scanning the forest. Brian, heart racing, thought he saw a glimmer of silver scales, there and gone.

Captain Sheehan stood still. Then he looked at Brian. "Thank you, my boy. You don't know, but—thank you. I suppose I've one fight left in me after all." His eyes were wet. "I didn't think I could. But I can. And then I'll go find Tommy."

"We need to get into the cabin," snapped Mr. Adler. "Come on—and block the door."

"Nay, don't go in," said Sheehan sharply. "Cabin's no more than a trap. Head due south. Do what my men tried to do. Take the boat." To Brian, "You've a compass, boy?"

There was one in the emergency kit. Brian nodded.

"We called it Goblin Cove—it's where my old girl sank," Sheehan went on. "Boat's in a cave, oars shipped."

The chiming of the fishhooks was getting louder. Closer.

Coco said, "We have to go!"

Sheehan said, "Now, miss, you just make straight for that cove. I don't know if I can kill the beastie. But I can slow her down. Then I'll be off. Wait for me, Tom."

And he hefted the massive axe, standing in front of the old cabin, and his face filled up with a fierce happiness. "Come on, you!" he shouted. "I'm brave enough for this. One more time."

Brian, turning, got a glimpse of shimmering scales before he dug out the compass.

South . . .

"This way!" he shouted, and ran. Heard the pounding feet as they all ran with him. And behind, in a voice shrill with laughter, he heard Captain Sheehan, of the *Goblin*, screaming insults at the snake.

Then silence, and they ran together, no one speaking, into the damp morning, while Brian consulted his compass and his shoes stuck in the mud of that cold and lonely island.

16

THERE WAS NO path across the island, of course. They climbed toward the summit anyway, shoving their way between trees. They were soon covered in clammy sweat, not a huge improvement from being cold.

None of them dared say very much. They were all listening. Even Ollie's dad wasn't cracking jokes. They crested a rise, finding themselves briefly scrambling on almost-bare rock, at the very top of the island, and then back down into trees. They didn't even look around, just put their heads down and kept doggedly on, as fast as they could.

The wind was rising. It riffled cold over their heads, over the rock, and over the trees. "Phil," said Mr. Adler once, abruptly, "what do you think of the haze? There, over the lake?"

Phil wiped his streaming nose and answered, "It usually means that the weather is changing."

"That's what I thought," said Ollie's dad. "Let's get on. Not that I want to put to sea—or lake—in a two-hundred-year-old boat, but I *really* don't want to do it in a thunderstorm."

None of them had said what they were really looking for, scanning the beaches, the trees, the water carefully, but Brian knew what it was. They all knew. They were looking for a silver flash, the streaking light of those beautiful, horrible scales.

Down the other side of the rise, out of the wind, and back into the shadows on the other side. This side of the island was steeper, the rocks more broken, and they all stumbled. Coco tripped and tripped again, until her shins were bleeding through her jeans.

On they went.

And on.

Hours seemed to pass. They were all exhausted. They didn't really dare stop. It was hard to know what time it was, but the shadows were definitely changing direction. Brian started to doubt his own reading of the compass.

Are we going in circles? he wondered.

How big can this island be?

Down and steadily down until they stood on a beach.

And there was no boat anywhere. Brian stared around him in the grayness—gray water, gray clouds gathering.

"The boat should be here," he said. "We kept going south. We went due south. Like Sheehan said. I'm *sure* of it. But where?"

"Welp," said Ollie's dad, practical and cheerful—the only one of them who was, at that point. "The log said a cave, right? Let's look around, shall we?"

"We'll find it," said Ollie, with a sudden, strange ferocity. "We're getting out of here."

And she glared at her watch as though she were talking to it. Mr. Adler looked down at her, frowning, but Ollie didn't look up, and after a second, as though the watch—the ghost of Ollie's mom—whatever animated the watch—was reluctant, the screen shifted and became a compass. But a very simple one that had two directions, N and F.

Near and Far, thought Brian.

"This way," said Ollie.

They wouldn't have found the boat at all, Brian thought, if it hadn't been for Ollie's watch. It was in a little rock cave, gouged in a bank of the beach and then walled up. The water had flooded in, murky, not once but a lot of times, and the outside of the boat's hull was slimy when they pulled it out.

It was also almost too heavy to lift, and so they had to collect sticks to make a path for it to the water. Brian wondered if they should have left their campsite earlier. They'd waited, avoiding the early morning. But the encounter with Sheehan and the walk across the island had taken way more time than Brian would have thought possible.

By the time they got the boat into the water, the sun was dropping, lower and lower.

But they got it into the water at last, and it floated. It didn't even leak; Phil had been right about the timbers swelling.

They couldn't find oars, however.

"But there's a mast, though," said Phil. "And we can use the emergency blanket and the rope from the *Cassie* as a sail."

"We need a boom," said Brian. "Can you sail it?"

Phil licked his lips, cracked and chapped like all of theirs were. "Yeah, bud," he said. "I think so."

"Let's call the boat the *Sheehan*," said Coco, and no one objected.

But it took longer than any of them wanted to rig the rope and the blanket so that it would hold, even a little, as a sail, and it was getting close to night before they finally pushed off. So far there was no sign of the snake. Maybe Sheehan had killed it, Brian thought. He'd probably killed it. Hadn't he?

The moon hung low in the sky, silvering the water, and all of them were shivering with the May cold.

The wind shoved them back onshore, and shoved them back again. "Just a little farther," panted Phil in frustration. "I think there's a breeze there—just rounding the point—you can see the ripple."

Finally, Ollie hopped out of the boat, teeth clenched and eyes wild, to her waist in freezing water, and began to shove the boat out, and her dad got out to help, and so did Ms. Zintner. They pushed until Ollie couldn't stand anymore, and her dad helped her back over the side of the *Sheehan*, and then he and Coco's mom pushed until he couldn't stand up in the water either, and by then they'd gone out quite a ways, and it was dead still, dead still over the water.

There were long moments of silence.

They all strained their eyes.

Nothing.

Then Brian felt a breeze on his cheek.

The sail rippled. And rippled again. Suddenly it bellied out, blocky against the sky, and Brian, inexperienced, jammed the tiller sideways, so that it almost went over. But someone must have known what they were doing when he built the boat in the first place, because it did not turn over.

"Orwell is due east," said Mr. Adler, through his chattering teeth.

"No," said Ollie. "Or, yes, it is, but not for us. Go around the point, Phil, and head for that fog."

"But—" said Phil.

"*Do it,*" chorused Ollie, Brian, and Coco, because through mist and water and through mirrors, that was how you went from world to world.

That was when they saw a silver shimmer in the water. It wasn't the moon, rising in the dusk.

Brian saw it first. "Guys!" he snapped. His voice came out strangled, if plenty loud. The silver shimmer swam like a snake, sinuous in the water.

There was no chance. No chance to dodge, no chance to avoid; they must only race, wind against monster, over the lake, toward the fog patch that might not even save them.

Ollie's face was set. Brian saw her measuring distances with her eyes. "You did promise," she whispered incomprehensibly.

For a second it seemed like the wind was going to save them. The lake monster was swimming slowly—so slowly—and there was something hesitant and stiff in the swaying of its silver coils. Definitely hurt. But it got closer. And closer.

They weren't going to make it.

Brian's mouth was dry as bone.

"How long?" Ollie demanded sharply, and this time Brian saw that she wasn't asking anyone in particular; instead she was looking straight down at the watch on her wrist.

The watch lit up. Coco saw the answer.

00:30:00 and then words, flashing in quick succession.

LOVE.

PROUD.

The snake bore down. The fog was closing. They were going to make it! No, they weren't.

Ollie suddenly shoved a piece of paper in Coco's hand. "I promised I wouldn't tell," she said. "He made me promise I wouldn't tell. But it's not the end. There's a chance. Okay?"

Coco stared at her friend in utter bewilderment, just as Ollie twisted around and jumped into the lake.

Coco screamed. She and Brian were on their feet together, Mr. Adler was turning, and all of them were shouting, "Ollie, *Ollie!*"

Nothing. The water had closed without a ripple over Ollie's head. Then she rose again; there was a splash and a check in the movement of the swimming lake monster.

Brian hadn't known he could scream that loud.

They shot into the fog, and they could see nothing.

It was like being in a cloud. Wet. A thick silence fell; Brian could feel his mouth moving, his throat working. He could see Coco doing the same, but no sound came out.

Then the boat slipped out of the fog again. The island had vanished. So had Ollie. But right before that, Brian could have sworn—always did swear, later— that he heard the unmistakable sound of someone laughing.

Out of the fog bank, everything had changed. There were the lights of Orwell, not that far away. The lake was still and quiet and icy cold. It stretched out to a vague unbroken horizon. No island. There was a faint smell of fish and of springtime earth. There was no sign of Ollie.

"Phil!" Brian snapped. "Mr. Adler! Come on, we have to go back, we have to save her!"

He was already digging the tiller into the water, threatening to send them into the lake. He was crying.

"Easy now," said Mr. Adler. "Brian, what's wrong?"

"Ollie!" he cried. "Didn't you see? Ollie got in the water—to keep the snake from getting us . . ."

Mr. Adler frowned. "Brian, I realize it's cold, and we're all super stressed, kiddo. Don't worry. We'll get inside soon. Wind's fair for Orwell."

"I—but." Coco was staring at Mr. Adler with a horrified incredulity that Brian knew was echoed on his own face. He realized that Coco was holding—clutching—Ollie's watch in her free hand, along with a ratty piece of paper. Her face was streaked with tears, the same tears that Brian could feel rolling down his own cheeks.

Brian leaned over and said, "What does the watch say?"

ALIVE

Brian felt himself breathe again.

"What's on the paper?"

He and Coco looked together. The lines were few and quickly scrawled:

He said I can't tell. So I won't.
But I bet with a few clues, you can guess.

1) Remember Jonathan?
2) He promised Dad wouldn't remember.
3) He wanted a rematch.
4) He always keeps his promises.

"Jonathan Webster," said Brian. "He made a deal with the smiling man to get his brother back from the dead. What did Ollie do?"

"She must have done it for her dad. To fix his hand," Coco whispered. "Made a bargain. That's what she wasn't telling us." Her body was shaking all over.

"But what'd she give him in exchange?" demanded Brian. "Did she jump in the lake to—to escape him?"

"No," said Coco. "She jumped because she knew he wouldn't let the snake kill her—because that's not what he promised. Not what she traded. So she's alive . . ."

Brian's heart beat fast with horror and with panic; he was cudgeling his brain as hard as it would go, trying to understand.

Something crinkled in his coat pocket. It hadn't been there before. Without thinking, he pulled out another piece of paper.

This one was thick and written in swirling, raised script. The same script that was on the black spot—the only warning they'd had. The warning of a day, a time, and a place.

It was a note.

Everyone has forgotten her, it said.

Except you.
You have one chance to win her back.
Call it a rematch.
I'll send an invitation. You'll know it when
you get it.

—S.

"The smiling man," said Brian. He didn't feel afraid at all anymore. Only furious—and glitteringly hopeful.

"One chance," said Coco.

"One chance is all we'll need," said Brian, and they looked grimly at each other as their wooden boat ground against the rocky shore and the moonlight silvered the water like the back of a dying monster.

Turn the page to see where Ollie, Coco,
and Brian's adventure began . . .

1

OCTOBER IN EAST EVANSBURG, and the last warm sun of the year slanted red through the sugar maples. Olivia Adler sat nearest the big window in Mr. Easton's math class, trying, catlike, to fit her entire body into a patch of light. She wished she were on the other side of the glass. You don't waste October sunshine. Soon the old autumn sun would bed down in cloud blankets, and there would be weeks of gray rain before it finally decided to snow. But Mr. Easton was teaching fractions and had no sympathy for Olivia's fidgets.

"Now," he said from the front of the room. His chalk squeaked on the board. Mike Campbell flinched. Mike Campbell got the shivers from squeaking blackboards and, for some reason, from people licking paper napkins. The sixth grade licked napkins around him as much as possible.

"Can anyone tell me how to convert three-sixteenths to a decimal?" asked Mr. Easton. He scanned the room for a victim. "Coco?"

"Um," said Coco Zintner, hastily shutting a sparkling pink notebook. "Ah," she added wisely, squinting at the board.

Point one eight seven five, thought Olivia idly, but she did not raise her hand to rescue Coco. She made a line of purple ink on her scratch paper, turned it into a flower, then a palm tree. Her attention wandered back to the window. *What if a vampire army came through the gates right now? Or no, it's sunny. Werewolves? Or what if the Brewsters' Halloween skeleton decided to unhook himself from the third-floor window and lurch out the door?*

Ollie liked this idea. She had a mental image of Officer Perkins, who got cats out of trees and filed police reports about pies stolen off windowsills, approaching a wandering skeleton. *I'm sorry, Mr. Bones, you're going to have to put your skin on—*

A large foot landed by her desk. Ollie jumped. Coco had either conquered or been conquered by three-sixteenths, and now Mr. Easton was passing out math quizzes. The whole class groaned.

"Were you paying attention, Ollie?" asked Mr. Easton, putting her paper on her desk.

"Yep," said Ollie, and added, a little at random, "point one eight seven five." Mr. Bones had failed to appear. Lazy skeleton. He could have gotten them out of their math quiz.

Mr. Easton looked unconvinced but moved on.

Ollie eyed her quiz. *Please convert 9/8 to a decimal. Right.* Ollie didn't use a calculator or scratch paper. The idea of using either had always puzzled her, as though someone had suggested she needed a spyglass to read a book. She scribbled answers as fast as her pencil could write, put her quiz on Mr. Easton's desk, and waited, half out of her seat, for the bell to ring.

Before the ringing had died away, Ollie seized her bag, inserted a crumpled heap of would-be homework, stowed a novel, and bolted for the door.

She had almost made it out when a voice behind her said, "Ollie."

Ollie stopped; Lily Mayhew and Jenna Gehrmann nearly tripped over her. Then the whole class was going around her like she was a rock in a river. Ollie trudged back to Mr. Easton's desk.

Why me, she wondered irritably. Phil Greenblatt had spent the last hour picking his nose and sticking boogers onto the seat in front of him. Lily had hacked her big sister's phone and screenshotted some texts Annabelle sent her boyfriend. The sixth grade had been giggling over them all day. And Mr. Easton wanted to talk to *her*?

Ollie stopped in front of the teacher's desk. "Yes? I turned in my quiz and everything so—"

Mr. Easton had a wide mouth and a large nose that drooped over his upper lip. A neatly trimmed mustache took up the tiny bit of space remaining. Usually he looked like a friendly walrus. Now he looked impatient. "Your quiz is letter-perfect, as you know, Ollie," he said. "No complaints on that score."

Ollie knew that. She waited.

"You should be doing eighth-grade math," Mr. Easton said. "At least."

"No," said Ollie.

Mr. Easton looked sympathetic now, as though he knew why she didn't want to do eighth-grade math. He probably did. Ollie had him for homeroom and life sciences, as well as math.

Ollie did not mind impatient teachers, but she did not like sympathy face. She crossed her arms.

Mr. Easton hastily changed the subject. "Actually, I wanted to talk to you about chess club. We're missing you this fall. The other kids, you know, really appreciated that you took the time to work with them on their opening gambits last year, and there's the interscholastic tournament coming up soon so—"

He went on about chess club. Ollie bit her tongue. She wanted to go outside, she wanted to ride her bike, and she didn't want to rejoin chess club.

When Mr. Easton finally came to a stop, she said, not quite meeting his eyes, "I'll send the club some links about opening gambits. Super helpful. They'll work fine. Um, tell everyone I'm sorry."

He sighed. "Well, it's your decision. But if you were to change your mind, we'd love—"

"Yeah," said Ollie. "I'll think about it." Hastily she added, "Gotta run. Have a good day. Bye." She was out the door before Mr. Easton could object, but she could feel him watching her go.

Past the green lockers, thirty-six on each side, down the hall that always smelled like bleach and old sandwiches. Out the double doors and onto the front lawn. All around was bright sun and cool air shaking golden trees: fall in East Evansburg. Ollie took a glad breath. She was going to ride her bike down along the creek as far and as fast as she could go. Maybe she'd jump in the water. The creek wasn't *that* cold. She would go home at dusk— sunset at 5:58. She had lots of time. Her dad would be mad that she got home late, but he was always worrying about something. Ollie could take care of herself.

Her bike was a Schwinn, plum-colored. She had locked it neatly to the space nearest the gate. No one in Evansburg would steal your bike—*probably*—but Ollie loved hers and sometimes people would prank you by stealing your wheels and hiding them.

She had both hands on her bike lock, tongue sticking out as she wrestled with the combination, when a shriek split the air. "It's *mine!*" a voice yelled. "Give it back! No—you can't touch that. NO!"

Ollie turned.

Most of the sixth grade was milling on the front lawn, watching Coco Zintner hop around like a flea— it was she who'd screamed. Coco would not have been out of place in a troop of flower fairies. Her eyes were large, slanting, and ice-blue. Her strawberry-blond hair was so strawberry that in the sunshine it looked pink. You could imagine Coco crawling out of a daffodil each morning and sipping nectar for breakfast. Ollie was a little jealous. She herself had a headful of messy brown curls and no one would ever mistake her for a flower fairy. *But at least,* Ollie reminded herself, *if Phil Greenblatt steals something from me, I'm big enough to sock him.*

Phil Greenblatt had stolen Coco's sparkly note-book. The one Coco had closed when Mr. Easton called on her. Phil was ignoring Coco's attempts to get it back—he was a foot taller than her. Coco was *tiny*. He held the notebook easily over Coco's head, flipped to the page he wanted, and snickered. Coco shrieked with frustration.

"Hey, Brian," called Phil. "Take a look at this."

Coco burst into tears.

Brian Battersby was the star of the middle school hockey team even though he was only twelve himself. He was way shorter than Phil, but looked like he fit together better, instead of sprouting limbs like a praying mantis. He was lounging against the brick wall of the school building, watching Phil and Coco with interest.

Ollie started to get mad. No one *liked* Coco much—she had just moved from the city and her squeaky enthusiasm annoyed everyone. But really, make her cry in school?

Brian looked at the notebook Phil held out to him. He shrugged. Ollie thought he looked more embar-rassed than anything.

Coco started crying harder.

Brian definitely looked uncomfortable. "Come on, Phil, it might not be me."

Mike Campbell said, elbowing Brian, "No, it's totally you." He eyed the notebook page again. "I guess it could be a dog that looks like you."

"Give it *back!*" yelled Coco through her tears. She snatched again. Phil was waving the notebook right over her head, laughing. The sixth grade was laughing too, and now Ollie could see what they were all looking at. It was a picture—a good picture, Coco could really draw—of Brian and Coco's faces nestled together with a heart around them.

Phil sat behind Coco in math class; he must have seen her drawing. Poor dumb Coco—why would you do that if you were sitting in front of nosy Philip Greenblatt?

"Come on, Brian," Mike was saying. "Don't you want to go out with Hot Cocoa here?"

Coco looked like she wanted to run away except that she really wanted her notebook back and Ollie had pretty much had enough of the whole situation, and so she bent down, got a moderate-sized rock, and let it fly.

Numbers and throwing things, those were the two talents of Olivia Adler. She'd quit the softball team last year too, but her aim was still on.

Her rock caught Brian squarely in the back of the head, dropped him *thump* onto the grass, and turned everyone's attention from Coco Zintner to her.

Ideally, Ollie would have hit Phil, but Phil was facing her and Ollie didn't want to put out an eye. Besides, she didn't have a lot of sympathy for Brian. He knew perfectly well that he was the best at hockey, and half the girls giggled about him, and he wasn't coming to Coco's rescue even though he'd more or less gotten her into this with his dumb friends and his dumb charming smile.

Ollie crossed her arms, thought in her mom's voice, *Well, in for a penny . . .* , hefted another rock, and said, "Oops. My hand slipped." The entire sixth grade was staring. The kids in front started backing away. A lot of them thought she had cracked since last year. "Um, seriously, guys," she said. "Doesn't *anyone* have anything better to do?"

Coco Zintner took advantage of Phil's distraction to snatch her notebook back. She gave Ollie a long look, and darted away.

Ollie thought, *I'm going to have detention for a year,* and then Brian got up, spitting out dirt, and said, "That was a pretty good throw."

The noise began. Ms. Mouton, that day's lawn monitor, finally noticed the commotion. "Now," she said, hurrying over. "Now, now." Ms. Mouton was the librarian and she was not the best lawn monitor.

Ollie decided that she wasn't going to say sorry or anything. Let them call her dad, let them shake their heads, let them give her detention tomorrow. At least tomorrow the weather would change and she would not be stuck in school on a nice day, answering questions.

Ollie jumped onto her bike and raced out of the school yard, wheels spitting gravel, before anyone could tell her to stop.

2

SHE PEDALED HARD past the hay bales in the round-
about on Main Street, turned onto Daisy Lane, and raced
past the clapboard houses, where jack-o'-lanterns grinned
on every front porch. She aimed her bike to knock down
a rotting gray rubber hand groping up out of the earth
in the Steiners' yard, turned again at Johnson Hill, and
climbed, panting, up the steep dirt road.

No one came after her. *Well, why would they,* Ollie
thought. She was Off School Property.

Ollie let her bike coast down the other side of
Johnson Hill. It was good to be alone in the warm
sunshine. The river ran silver to her right, chattering
over rocks. The fire-colored trees shook their leaves
down around her. It wasn't *hot,* exactly—but warm for
October. Just cool enough for jeans, but the sun was
warm when you tilted your face to it.

The swimming hole was Ollie's favorite place. Not far from her house, it had a secret spot on a rock half-hidden by a waterfall. That spot was *Ollie's*, especially on fall days. After mid-September, she was the only one who went there. People didn't go to swimming holes once the weather turned chilly.

Other than her homework, Ollie was carrying *Captain Blood* by Rafael Sabatini, a broken-spined paperback that she'd dug out of her dad's bookshelves. She mostly liked it. Peter Blood outsmarted everyone, which was a feature she liked in heroes, although she wished Peter were a girl, or the villain were a girl, or *someone* in the book besides his boat and his girlfriend (both named Arabella) were a girl. But at least the book had romance and high-seas adventures and other *absolutely not Evansburg* things. Ollie liked that. Reading it meant going to a new place where she wasn't Olivia Adler at all.

Ollie braked her bike. The ground by the road was carpeted with scarlet leaves; sugar maples start losing their leaves before other trees. Ollie kept a running list in her head of sugar maples in Evansburg that didn't belong to anyone. When the sap ran, she and her mom would—

Nope. No, they wouldn't. They could buy maple syrup.

The road that ran beside the swimming hole looked like any other stretch of road. A person just driving by wouldn't know the swimming hole was there. But, if you knew just where to look, you'd see a skinny dirt trail that went from the road to the water. Ollie walked her bike down the trail. The trees seemed to close in around her. Above was a white-railed bridge. Below, the creek paused in its trip down the mountain. It spread out, grew deep and quiet enough for swimming. There was a cliff for jumping and plenty of hiding places for one girl and her book. Ollie hurried. She was eager to go and read by the water and be alone.

The trees ended suddenly, and Ollie was standing on the bank of a cheerful brown swimming hole.

But, to her surprise, someone was already there.

A slender woman, wearing jeans and flannel, stood at the edge of the water.

The woman was sobbing.

Maybe Ollie's foot scuffed a rock, because the woman jumped and whirled around. Ollie gulped. The woman was pretty, with amber-honey hair. But she had circles under her eyes like purple thumbprints. Streaks of mascara had run down her face, like she'd been crying for a while.

"Hello," the woman said, trying to smile. "You surprised me." Her white-knuckled hands gripped a small, dark thing.

"I didn't mean to scare you," Ollie said cautiously.

Why are you crying? she wanted to ask. But it seemed impolite to ask that question of a grown-up, even if her face was streaked with the runoff from her tears.

The woman didn't reply; she darted a glance to the rocky path by the creek, then back to the water. Like she was looking out for something. Or someone.

Ollie felt a chill creep down her spine. She said, "Are you okay?"

"Of course." The woman tried to smile again. Fail. The wind rustled the leaves. Ollie glanced behind her. Nothing.

"I'm fine," said the woman. She turned the dark thing over in her hands. Then she said, in a rush, "I just have to get rid of this. Put it in the water. And then—" The woman broke off.

Then? What then? The woman held the thing out over the water. Ollie saw that it was a small black book, the size of her spread-out hand.

Her reaction was pure reflex. "You can't throw away a book!" Ollie let go of her bike and jumped forward. Part of her wondered, *Why would you come here to throw a book in the creek? You can donate a book.* There were donation boxes all over Evansburg.

"I have to!" snapped the woman, bringing Ollie up short. The woman went on, half to herself, "That's the bargain. Make the arrangements. Then give the book to the water." She gave Ollie a pleading look. "I don't have a choice, you see."

Ollie tried to drag the conversation out of crazy town. "You can donate a book if you don't want it," she said firmly. "Or—or give it to someone. Don't just throw it in the creek."

"I *have* to," said the woman again.

"Have to drop a book in the creek?"

"Before tomorrow," said the woman. Almost to herself, she whispered, "Tomorrow's the day."

Ollie was nearly within arm's reach now. The woman smelled sour—frightened. Ollie, completely bewildered, decided to ignore the stranger elements of the conversation. Later, she would wish she hadn't. "If you don't want that book, I'll take it," said Ollie. "I like books."

The woman shook her head. "He said water. Upstream. Where Lethe Creek runs out of the mountain. I'm here. I'm *doing* it!" She shrieked the last sentence as though someone besides Ollie were listening. Ollie had to stop herself from looking behind her again.

"Why?" she asked. Little mouse feet crept up her spine.

"Who knows?" the woman whispered. "Just his game, maybe. He enjoys what he does, you know, and that is why he's always smiling—" She smiled too, a joyless pumpkin-head grin.

Ollie nearly yelped. But instead, her hand darted up and she snatched the book. It felt fragile under her fingers, gritty with dust. Surprised at her own daring, Ollie hurriedly backed up.

The woman's face turned red. "Give that back!" A glob of spit hit Ollie in the cheek.

"I don't think so," said Ollie. "You don't want it anyway." She was backing toward her bike, half expecting the woman to fling herself forward.

The woman was staring at Ollie as if really seeing her for the first time. "Why—?" A horrified understanding dawned on her face that Ollie didn't understand. "How old are you?"

Ollie was still backing toward her bike. "Eleven," she answered, by reflex. Almost there . . .

"Eleven?" the woman breathed. "Eleven. Of course, eleven." Ollie couldn't tell if the woman was giggling or crying. Maybe both. "It's his kind of joke—" She broke off, leaned forward to whisper. "Listen to me, Eleven. I'm going to tell you one thing, because I'm not a bad person. I just didn't have a choice. I'll give you some advice, and you give me the book." She had her hand out, fingers crooked like claws.

Ollie, poised on the edge of flight, said, "Tell me what?" The creek rushed and rippled, but the harsh sounds of the woman's breathing were louder than the water.

"Avoid large places at night," the woman said. "Keep to small."

"Small?" Ollie was torn between wanting to run and wanting to understand. "That's it?"

"Small!" shrieked the woman. *"Small spaces! Keep to small spaces or see what happens to you! Just see!"* She burst into wild laughter. The plastic witch sitting on the Brewsters' porch laughed like that. *"Now give me that book!"* Her laughter turned into a whistling sob.

Ollie heaved the Schwinn around and fled with it up the trail. The woman's footsteps scraped behind. "Come back!" she panted. "Come back!"

Ollie was already on the main road, her leg thrown over the bike's saddle. She rode home as fast as she could, bent low over her handlebars, hair streaming in the wind, the book lying in her pocket like a secret.

The creepy, spine-tingling
adventure continues in . . .

1

WINTER IN EAST EVANSBURG, and just after dusk, five people in a beat-up old Subaru peeled out of town in a snowstorm. Snow and road salt flew up from their tires as they got on the highway heading north. The five were nearly the only people on the road. *"A major winter storm is blanketing parts of northern Vermont with eight inches overnight . . ."* said the radio, crackling. *"Be advised that the roads are dangerous."*

The Subaru kept going. In front were two adults. In the back were three kids.

Coco Zintner sat in the middle of the back seat, because she was the smallest. She was short and skinny, her eyes blue, her hair (Coco's favorite thing about herself) an odd pinkish blond. Coco peered nervously through the windshield. The road looked slippery.

They were going to spend the next three hours driving on it.

"Awesome," said the girl to Coco's left. Her name was Olivia Adler. She was Coco's best friend, and she wasn't nervous at all. "Eight inches overnight." She pressed her nose to the car window. She had big dark eyes and the kind of corkscrewing curls that couldn't ever be brushed, because they'd frizz. She stared out at the snowstorm with delight. "We're going to have so much fun tomorrow."

Coco's other best friend, the boy on Coco's right, grinned back at Ollie. The Subaru's storage area was piled high with bags. He reached into the jumble and patted his green ski boots. "It's gonna be *lit*," he said. "Don't look so nervous, Tiny."

That was to Coco. She scowled. Brian gave nearly everyone a nickname. She liked Brian, but she hated her nickname. Probably because she was actually kind of tiny. Brian had the best smile of anyone Coco knew. He'd been born in Jamaica, but his parents had moved to Vermont when he was a baby. He was black, not particularly tall, and the star of the middle school hockey team. He loved books as much as he loved scoring goals, and even though he could sometimes act like a dumb hockey player, Brian was good at noticing what went on around him.

Like the fact that Coco was nervous. She wished he wouldn't tease her about it.

It was the first day of winter break, and the five of them were going skiing: Ollie and Brian and Coco, plus Ollie's dad (who was driving) and Coco's mom (who was riding shotgun).

Neither adult could really afford a week of skiing. Coco's mother was a journalist, and Ollie's father sold solar panels. But the month before, Ollie's dad had come home from work smiling.

"What?" Ollie had asked. She and Coco were sitting in the kitchen of the Egg, Ollie's rambling old farmhouse. They'd gotten themselves mugs of hot chocolate and were seeing who could build the biggest marshmallow pyramid on top.

Mr. Adler just grinned. "Want to go skiing over the winter holiday?"

"Huh?" said both girls in chorus.

Turned out Ollie's dad had won a prize. For selling a lot of solar panels. A week for him and four others at Mount Hemlock.

"Mount Hemlock?" Ollie had asked, stunned. "But it's not even open yet!"

Mount Hemlock was Vermont's newest ski mountain. It had never been open to the public before. Some school had owned it. But now it had new owners, who were turning the mountain into a winter getaway.

"Yep," said Mr. Adler happily. "They're hosting a few people over the holiday, before the official opening. Want to go? Coco? Do you and your mom want to go?"

Coco had only learned to ski that winter, and still thought that sliding fast down a mountain was cold and scary. She wasn't sure if she wanted to go. But Ollie was already doing a happy dance around the house, and Coco didn't want to disappoint her.

"Sure," she said in a small voice. "Yeah, I'll go."

Now they were actually in the car, actually going, and Coco had butterflies in her stomach, thinking of the storm, the slippery road, the big cold mountain at the end of it. She wished they were still back at Ollie's house, in front of Bernie the woodstove, making marshmallow pyramids. The wind whipped snow across the windshield.

Coco told Brian, in a voice that probably fooled no one, "I'm not nervous about *skiing*." She waved a hand at the windshield. "I'm nervous about driving in a snowstorm."

"Well," said Mr. Adler calmly from the front, "technically, *I'm* driving in a snowstorm." He changed gears on the Subaru. His hair was as dark as Ollie's,

4

though it was straight instead of curly. For the winter, he'd grown out a giant reddish beard. *Keeps me warm,* he would say.

"You're doing amazing, Dad," Ollie said. "You and Susie." Susie was the Subaru. "Dad's driven through a lot of snowstorms," she said to Coco reassuringly. "All fine."

The streetlights disappeared a little outside of Evansburg, and it was dark on the road except for their headlights.

"It's okay, Tiny," said Brian. "We probably won't slide into a ditch."

"Probably?" Coco asked.

"Definitely," said Coco's mom from the passenger seat. She turned back to give Brian a stern look. Brian played innocent. Coco and her mom had the exact same blue eyes, though her mom was tall instead of tiny, and her hair was blond, not pinkish. Coco kept hoping for a growth spurt.

"If we do slide into a ditch," said Ollie, "you get to push us out, Brian."

"Naw," said Brian. "You're bigger than me. You push us out."

Coco interrupted. "You both can push us out. Are there any snacks?"

That distracted all three of them. It was dinner-time, and there were snacks. Mr. Adler was a specialist in snacks. He'd made them each a large peanut-butter-and-jelly sandwich on homemade bread.

After they'd finished their sandwiches, they each ate an apple and shared a big bag of potato chips. Mr. Adler had made the chips too.

"Is it *hard* to make potato chips?" Coco asked dis-believingly, licking salt off her fingers.

"No," said Ollie, in a superior tone. She'd helped make them. Also, Coco suspected, eaten a lot of them before the drive even started. "But the oil splashes."

"I know what we're making next time we're at your house," said Brian, crunching. "These are *amazing*."

They were scuffling over the last of the potato chips when the Subaru finally turned off the main highway. MOUNTAIN ACCESS ROAD, said a sign. The road tilted steeply up. On one side were trees. On the other side was a gully and a frozen creek. Ollie's dad was driving on through the storm like he didn't have a care in the world, telling bad jokes from the front seat.

"What did the buffalo say to his kid when he dropped him off at school?" he asked.

Ollie sighed. Her dad *loved* bad jokes.

"Bison!" yelped Coco triumphantly, and everyone groaned but also laughed.

"Motorists are warned to exercise caution, avoid unplowed roads, and, if at all possible, refrain from driving altogether," remarked the radio.

"Great," said Mr. Adler, unbothered. "Less people on the road tonight means more snow for us tomorrow!"

"If you say so," said Coco's mom. She gave the smothering storm a cautious look. Coco recognized the look. Coco and her mom were both careful about things. Unlike Ollie and her dad, who were kind of leap-before-you-look.

"Want to hear another joke?" Mr. Adler asked.

"Dad, can't we have a jokes-per-trip limit?" Ollie said.

"Not when I'm driving!" said her dad. "One more. Why did the scarecrow get a promotion?"

A small, awkward silence fell. Ollie, Brian, and Coco looked at each other. They *really* didn't like scarecrows.

"Anyone?" asked Ollie's dad. "Anyone? Come on, I feel like I'm talking to myself here! Because he was *outstanding in his field*! Get it? Out standing in his field?" Ollie's dad laughed, but no one laughed with him. "Geez, tough crowd."

The three in the back said nothing. Ollie's dad didn't know it, but there was a reason they didn't like scarecrows.

That October, they, along with the rest of their sixth-grade class, had disappeared for two days. Only

Ollie, Brian, and Coco remembered everything that had happened during those days. They'd never told anyone. They told their families and the police that they'd gotten lost.

They hadn't just gotten lost. But who would believe them if they told the truth?

They'd been kidnapped into another world. A world behind the mist. They'd met living scarecrows who tried to drag them off and turn them into scarecrows too. They'd gone into a haunted house, taken food from a ghost, run a corn maze, and at last met someone called the smiling man.

The smiling man looked ordinary, but he wasn't. The smiling man would grant your heart's desire if you asked him. But he'd demand a price. A terrible price.

Ollie, Brian, and Coco had outwitted the smiling man. They'd survived the world behind the mist and come home. They'd gone into that world as near strangers and come out as best friends. It was December now, and they were together, and on vacation. All was well.

But two months later, they still had nightmares. And they still didn't like scarecrows.

The silence in the car stretched out as the road got even steeper. The radio suddenly fizzed with static and went silent.

They all waited for it to crackle back to life. Nothing. Coco's mom reached out and tapped it, pressed the tuning button, but it didn't help. "That's weird," she said. "Maybe it's the storm."

Coco didn't miss the radio. She was full of peanut butter and getting sleepy. She leaned her head on Ollie's shoulder to doze. Brian was reading *Voyage of the Dawn Treader*. Brian liked sea stories. He and Ollie had both read one called *Captain Blood* and spent a few weeks arguing about the ending. Coco had read the book too, to know what her friends were arguing about, but it was about pirates. She hadn't liked it and felt a little left out of the whole argument. Coco didn't like novels, really. She liked books about real things. Bugs and dinosaurs and the history of space flight.

Brian began to read by the light of his phone. Ollie put her cheek against her window and stared into the wild night. Coco, half asleep on Ollie's shoulder, began recalling the last chess game she'd played. It was on the internet, with someone named @begemot.

Coco loved chess. Her favorite books were histories of famous players and famous matches. One of her favorite things to do was to play online. On the internet, no one could be smug and assume she was easy to beat just because she was small and pink-haired. Sleepily,

Coco went back over the opening moves of her last game. She'd played white, which always goes first, and had opened with Queen's Gambit . . .

Up and up they climbed.

Coco fell asleep, still thinking about chess.

Coco dreamed. Not about chess.

In her dream, she was walking down a dark hallway, so long that she couldn't see the end of it. Bars of moonlight fell across the carpet, striping it with shadows. But there weren't any windows. Just the moonlight. It was bitterly cold. On each side were rows of plain white doors, the paint rotten and peeling. Behind one of the doors, Coco heard someone crying.

But behind which door? There seemed to be hundreds. "Where are you?" Coco called.

"I can't find them," whimpered a girl's voice. "I've looked everywhere, but I can't find them. Mother says I can't go home until I find them."

Coco thought she heard footsteps plodding along behind her. Heavy, uneven footsteps. Her skin started to crawl. But she had to find the crying girl. She was sure of it. She had to find her before the footsteps caught up. She ran along faster. "What are you looking for?" she called. "I can help you find it. Where are you?"

Then she lurched to a halt. A skinny girl, about her own height, dressed in a white nightgown, had appeared in the hallway. Her face was in shadow. "Here," the girl said.

For some reason, Coco did not want to see the girl's face. "Hello?" she said, hearing her voice crack.

"I'm looking for my bones," whispered the girl. "Can you help me?"

She moved into the light. Coco flinched. The other girl was gray-faced and skinny. Her eyes were two blank pits. Her lips and nose were black, like she had terrible frostbite. She tried, horribly, to smile. "Hello," she said. "It's cold here, isn't it? Won't you help me?" She reached out a single hand. Her fingernails were long and black in the moonlight.

Coco, stumbling backward, ran into something solid. A huge hand fell on her shoulder. Coco whirled and looked up into the face of a scarecrow. Its sewn-on mouth was smiling wide. Its hand wasn't a hand at all, just a sharp garden trowel. It had found her at last, Coco thought. It had found her, and now it was going to drag her off. She'd never get home again . . .

Coco opened her mouth to scream, and woke up with a gasp.

She was in the car, in the snowstorm, driving to Mount Hemlock, and her mother was talking to Mr. Adler in the front seat. It was cold in the back seat; her toes in their winter boots were numb. Coco sat still for a second, breathing fast with fright. *Just a dream*, she told herself. She'd had a lot of scarecrow dreams in the last few months. So had Ollie and Brian. *Just a dream.*

"How much farther, Roger?" Coco's mom asked.

"Should be pretty close now," said Mr. Adler.

Coco, a little dazed from her nightmare, stared out the front windshield. It was snowing even harder. The road was a thin yellowish-white strip, piled thick with snow. More snow bowed the trees on either side.

The Subaru was moving slowly. The thick snow groaned under the wheels, and Mr. Adler seemed to be struggling to keep the car going straight on the slippery road. "What a night, huh?" he said.

"Want me to drive?" asked Coco's mom.

This time the usual cheer was gone from Mr. Adler's reply. "It's okay. I know the car better." Lower, he added, "Just pray we don't get stuck."

Now the car was coming down into a gully, the road turning slightly.

But the road wasn't empty. For a stomach-clenching second, Coco thought she was still dreaming. Right in front of them, in the middle of the road, stood a tall figure in a ragged blue ski jacket. It looked like a scarecrow. The figure was perfectly still. One palm was raised and turned out as though to beg. As though to say, *STOP*. The face was hidden by a ski mask.

Coco felt a jolt of terror. But then she realized that the person had real hands. Not garden tools. She wasn't dreaming; this wasn't a scarecrow.

Mr. Adler wasn't slowing down. "Stop!" yelled Coco, yanking herself upright. "Look! *Look!*"

Mr. Adler slammed on the brakes. The car skidded, turning sideways, swinging them toward the thick black ranks of trees. Coco braced, waiting to hear the thump of someone slamming into the side of the car. The person had been *so close* . . .

Nothing.

The car shuddered to a stop, only a couple feet from the nearest tree trunk.

All of them sat stunned for a second.

"I didn't feel us hit anything." Mr. Adler sounded like he was taking deep breaths, trying to be calm. "What did you see, Coco?"

Coco was startled. "You didn't see it? There was a person in the road! We must have hit him!" Her voice sounded squeaky. She hated when her voice sounded squeaky. Had they hurt someone? Had they *killed* . . .

Ollie's dad put on the emergency brake and turned on the car's hazard lights. "Kids, I need you to stay—"

he began, but Ollie had already unlocked her door and scrambled out into the snow. It came up to her knees. Brian was right behind her on his side, and Coco, although her hands were shaking, hurried after them.

"Coco!" cried her mom as she and Mr. Adler followed. "Coco, don't look, get back, be careful—"

Coco pretended not to hear. She grabbed her phone, went around the car, and shined the light at the snow. Brian was doing the same. Ollie had pulled a headlamp from the pocket on her car door. The three of them stood shoulder to shoulder, shining their flashlights all around the car. The snow was falling so thickly that they couldn't see anything outside the circle of their lights. Faintly, Coco heard the whisper of wind in the pine needles overhead.

Mr. Adler had a flashlight from the glove compartment. Coco's mom stood next to him, squinting into the snowstorm. Four beams of light shone on the snow. The road was utterly empty. Coco saw the tracks where the car had come down, saw the huge sideways mark of the car's skid. But nothing else.

"I don't see anyone. Any tracks, even," said her mom. "Thank god."

"But I *saw* someone," protested Coco. "In the road. A person. They had their hand out." She raised her own arm, palm out, to demonstrate. "They were wearing a blue ski jacket, but no gloves. Ollie, did you see?"

"I thought I might have seen something," said Ollie. She sounded doubtful. "Like a shadow. But I wasn't sure. There's so much snow. Brian?"

Brian shook his head. "But," he said loyally, "Ollie and I couldn't see out the windshield as well as Coco, since she was in the middle."

Coco's mom gestured at the snow, which was unmarked except for the car's tracks and their own footprints. "I don't think there was anyone here." She started to shiver. They'd all taken off their heavy coats for driving, and now the snow was piling up on their shoulders.

"I *saw* someone," Coco insisted, but the others, eager to get back into the warm car, weren't listening anymore. She hurried after them. "I definitely saw someone."

"It might have just been a shadow, Tiny," said Brian reasonably. "Or a deer. Or maybe you were just dreaming and you mixed up being asleep and being awake."

"I wasn't imagining things!" cried Coco, wishing *so hard* that her voice wouldn't squeak. "And don't call me Tiny!"

"But there's obviously no one—" Brian began.

"Hey," said Ollie's dad, cutting them off. "Easy now, both of you. Just be glad we didn't hit anyone. Let's get back in the car. It's not safe here."

Coco climbed unhappily back into the car. She felt like everyone was just a little bit mad at her for yelling *stop* so that Mr. Adler had to slam on his brakes and send them skidding dangerously across the road. She was *sure* she'd seen someone.

But she *had* been half asleep. Maybe she did dream it.

As they drove away, Coco turned around and looked out the back window.

Just for a second, she thought she saw a dark figure lit red by the car's rear lights. It stood facing them in the middle of the road. One bare hand was still upraised.

Like a plea.

Like a warning.

"Guys," she whispered. "It's there. It's *right back there*."

Ollie and Brian turned around.

There was a small silence.

"I don't see anything," said Ollie.

Coco looked again.

The figure was gone.

Coco shivered. She opened her mouth to say something else. But before she could, the car was grumbling up the mountain once more and they had left the gully behind them.

A minute later, two yellow lights shone through the trees. Maybe it was just because Coco was shaken up, but she thought that the lights looked sinister. Like eyes peeping. Waiting for them. She wanted to tell Mr. Adler to turn the car around.

Don't be silly, she told herself.

"Look!" said Brian, pointing. "What's that?"

"Must be the lodge," said Mr. Adler. He sounded relieved. "We're almost there."

They drove under a new, hand-carved sign lit by two old-fashioned gas lamps.

Eyes? Right, Coco thought. *Just lamps.*

MOUNT HEMLOCK RESORT, said the sign. A MOUNTAIN OF AWESOME WHERE WINTER NEVER ENDS.

"That's some weird grammar," commented Ollie.

No one said anything else. The resort drive was the narrowest road they'd driven on, and the most thickly piled with snow. The Subaru's motor whined horribly as Ollie's dad pushed down the accelerator. The driveway turned, and the car skidded slowly sideways, almost going into a spin. The wheels couldn't bite.

"Dad—" Ollie began.

"Not now!" snapped her father in a tone Coco had never heard from Mr. Adler. He changed gears, managed to keep the car from skidding, and then they burst out from the driveway into a snow-covered parking lot. Everyone breathed a huge sigh of relief.

After the long, cold drive, the sight of Hemlock Lodge was like Christmas morning. Warm golden light blazed out of the windows. Well, some of the windows.

"We made it," said Brian happily.

They could barely see the building in the snowy darkness, but Coco thought it was big. It had a— presence. It loomed over them.

"Shouldn't there be more lights?" asked Ollie.

"Power must be out," said Coco's mom. She tugged the end of her blond braid, considering. "They're running on generators. Can't light everything."

"I can hear the generators," said Brian.

Mr. Adler drove across the parking lot and parked under an awning. Coco could hear the generators too: a slow, roaring noise, like the building was breathing.

"Well," said Mr. Adler, "parking lot's empty. Looks like we were the only ones to make the drive."

"There might be others stuck on the road somewhere," said Coco's mom. "Hopefully they get to shelter.

Another hour, and we'd have gotten stuck ourselves. Next time let's listen to what the radio has to say about snowstorms, hm?"

"Deal," said Ollie's dad, and he sounded like he really meant it. "Come on!" he added to all of them. "We made it, all present and accounted for. Grab a bag. The sooner we get out, the sooner we get to bed."

Ollie and Brian fumbled for the door handles and stumbled into the freezing night. All of them padded sleepily into Hemlock Lodge.

Coco stopped dead right in the entrance, staring. Ollie plowed into Coco and had to catch her so they both didn't fall. "Coco, what—" she began, and then she saw what Coco had. "No way."

"Holy cow," muttered Brian. "Where are we?"

The only light in the lobby was from a big, roaring fire. Shadows leaped and swung across the walls; you couldn't even see the ceiling. But the walls were completely covered with heads. Dead animal heads. Coco spotted a moose head with Christmas lights wound through its antlers. A deer head—a lot of deer heads— hung in a cluster. There was a trio of raccoons in a small canoe with paddles. A stuffed fawn in a glass box. Four coyotes looked like they were howling at a fake moon. A black bear stood on its hind legs, its paw upraised.

In the flickering firelight, they seemed to move; their glass eyes shone like they were alive. The bear had sharp white teeth.

"Nice decorations," said Brian uneasily. "Great spot your dad found." There was a giant bearskin rug on the floor. Its claws were shiny in the firelight.

Ollie stepped around Coco and marched into the lobby. "It's great," she said pointedly. Ollie always defended her dad. Coco would have too, if she'd had a dad as cool as Ollie's. Coco had never met her dad. He'd left before Coco was born.

Ollie waved at the heads. "Some people like this kind of thing. And we're not here to hang out in the lobby, we're here to ski."

Brian brightened. "Yes, we are," he said. His green ski boots were draped over his backpack; he reached behind and patted them again. Brian loved all gear, for all sports. Especially his own gear. He and Ollie would go on endlessly about tuning skis and sharpening ice skates. Sometimes Coco wished that she liked the things her friends liked. Pirate books and winter stuff. She'd have more to say when they were talking.

Two people, a man and a woman, had been standing by the front desk, waiting for them. Now they hurried forward, clattering across the lodge. They were smiling, freckled, happy. Coco was really glad to see them. They made the lobby seem a lot more normal.

"Oh, you made it, I'm so glad!" said the woman. She was thin as a greyhound, sandy-haired, with *cheery welcome* written all over her face like she'd painted it there. "You must be Roger Adler," she said to Ollie's dad. "I'm Sue Wilson. You're the first guests to arrive—a lot of them probably didn't set out at all! *What* a storm! Sorry about the dark." She waved a hand at the lobby. "We thought the fire would be enough. Electricity's out, and we're trying to save on propane in case we're snowed in for a couple of days. Plenty of firewood, though!" She turned to the kids. "You can call me Sue." She smiled at Coco. "You tired, hon?"

Coco was used to adults calling her *hon, sweetie,* and *darling.* Adults who didn't know her mostly seemed to think she was about eight years old. It was the pinkish hair. She *really* wished she'd get that growth spurt.

"Yes," she said politely, gritting her teeth. "I am. What happened to the electricity?"

"The storm," said the man, coming forward. "Wind blew trees over the power lines somewhere or other." He had a beard as big as Mr. Adler's and wore a Christmas sweater. A little belly hung over his belt. "I'm Sam Wilson," he said. "Me 'n' Sue own the place.

Pleased to meet you. I guess you saw my little critters."
He waved a hand at the wall. "Bagged 'em all myself!
Lemme take those." He swept up all three of their duffels before they could respond. "Now," he said. "Enough chitchat. You must be tired. Stairs are this way. Sorry the elevator's not working. Power's out and all. Come on. Welcome to Hemlock Lodge."

Coco followed him gratefully, glad to get to bed and away from the animal heads.

"Big storm out there, Sue," Coco heard Mr. Adler saying. "Should make for some good skiing tomorrow, but it was a tough drive." He raised his voice. "Good night, kids! Be good."

The adults kept on talking, but Coco couldn't hear what they were saying. She padded up the stairs with the others.

They stopped on the second floor. The stairs opened onto a long dim hall. The only light was from a few wide-spaced wall lamps. They cast pools of feeble yellow light. *Must be part of saving on propane,* Coco decided, *keeping it so dark.* She tripped over the last step and lurched into Ollie, who was weighed down by her own backpack and nearly went over.

"Coco!" whispered Ollie. She didn't usually get mad when Coco was clumsy, but they were all really tired.

"Sorry," Coco whispered back. "It's hard to see."

They began the long trudge down the hall. Coco watched her feet carefully, trying not to trip again. "I've got you girls in the bunk room," Sam called over his shoulder. "You"—Brian was it—"are right across the hall. Far end of the hallway. Follow me."

The hall seemed to go on forever. It was chilly. Coco hoped their room was warmer.

Sam stopped at a door that said BUNK ROOM in big brass letters.

Behind her, Coco heard more footsteps coming up the stairs, shuffling along behind them. Must be her mom and Mr. Adler, going to their rooms. Coco looked back. "Good night, Mo—" she started to say.

But her mom wasn't there. The hall was empty.

No—what was that? Near them was a pool of greenish light, thrown from one of the dim emergency bulbs. Cast across the light was a person's shadow. A big broad-shouldered shadow.

One shadow-hand was stretched out toward them.

Like a plea.

Like a warning.

A chill ran down her spine. "Mom?" Coco called just as their door swung open; Sam flicked on a battery-powered lamp. Light flooded the hall, and the shadow vanished. There was *definitely* no one there.

Coco thought then of the strange figure in the road and, for some reason, of the long hallway in her dream.

Her heart beating uncomfortably fast, Coco followed Ollie into the bunk room.

Acknowledgments

WRITING BOOKS IS like spending your life on group projects, and I am always grateful to the many people who bring my books into existence. Thanks in particular to Paul Lucas and Eloy Bleifus, to Stacey Barney and Caitlin Tutterow, to Evan Johnson, Garrett Welson, RJ Adler, and Pollaidh Major, to Cassandra Brett and Joe Coppa, and to the many, many educators, parents, and students who have picked up these books and read them aloud in the dark. May there be many more.